ISBN-10: 0985741716

ISBN-13: 978-0-9857417-1-6

Library of Congress Control Number: 2013921114

Pressea Publishing, Garden Grove, CA

Outlander Leander: Vol.2

Coronation Necklace

By:
Eisah

Edited by:
Laurie Laliberte of the Kindle All-Stars

Illustrations by:
Silvia Texidó Viyuela [Lylith]

Table of Contents

My eyes darted back and forth, waiting for decrepit hands to lunge out and grab me from the mist. Even abandoned, history forever tainted the city.

I stood in the middle of what used to be a park. In front of me, a mechanical crystal tree still reached for the sky. Dozens of branches sprouted from the trunk, each with a series of crystals hanging from varying lengths of string. Even after decades of neglect, it was obvious that this used to be a brilliant spectacle, a masterpiece of engineering and art. Now webs and dirt soiled it.

Kneeling down by a panel on the front, my fingers hovered over the switches. I flipped one in the top corner and the tree came to life with a whirr.

The branches creaked along in a circular motion and the crystals rang against a bar in sequence. Low murmuring from the gears inside added to the music. Missing and broken chimes left the cheerful tune hollow. The music wasn't quite right. Nothing about the city was.

Wilten Crags. Every Naggian knew the basic story of this city, even me. About forty years before, a group of scientists experimented on people. It got so out of control that when the government found out, they evacuated the city and sealed it off. Every scientist involved was executed save for one who managed to escape before the soldiers arrived. The lone scientist

still clawed his way through popular scary stories.

Walls surrounded the city; no one came and no one went.

The government didn't do anything to keep people out of Wilten Crags. People who believed in ghosts stayed away out of fear. People who didn't believe in ghosts stayed away just in case they were wrong.

Then there was me, the idiot who got talked into coming here to collect tokens of a tragedy most wanted to forget.

Ghosts aren't real, I repeated the mantra in my head. Being here challenged my skepticism, no matter how much I reassured myself. A fog hovered over the broken-down city as if even Pressea herself wanted to hide its existence. *It's a valley. Of course fog is hanging around,* I tried to ease my nerves. I knew better. After forty years, even if the scientist was still alive, he'd be elderly. I could fight him off. And he'd have run far from here by now. If he was alive.

A shriek from the tree pierced my thoughts and I gritted my teeth. My hands flew to my ears before swatting at the switchboard. The tree ground to a halt with a screech as I winced. When I opened my eyes the shimmer of a crystal lying on the ground caught my attention. I pinched the severed cord still attached to it and held it up. The cord was frayed and the crystal was dirty, but it still twinkled when held up to the light.

I stuffed it into my bag and glared at the city behind me. This wasn't the type of treasure I wanted to hunt. No, these were mementos for people obsessed with the horrors that happened here. Ellora sent me here once before, and I knew the first time that it was my least favorite place in the world.

While I walked down the street, I pulled out a pocket phone I got for emergencies and called the only person I used it for thus far.

Ellora's face popped up on the flat screen, lips pursed together. "I told you not to call me here. Talk to Galloughs."

I had my own nasty glare for her. "I need to talk to you! I hate this place!"

"Don't tell me you're scared," she sneered as she looked down her nose at me.

"You haven't been here." My eyes darted about while I walked the barren streets.

"Is the big bad scientist going to get you?"

"Ellora!"

She lifted a hand in a partial shrug, shaking her head. "Relax. That place has been abandoned longer than you've been alive."

"Then why don't you come here next time?" I challenged her.

"If I went then what would I need to keep you around for?"

"I don't care! I didn't sign up for this. I'm sick of looking for creepy souvenirs!"

"Do you think information about artifacts gets posted on the news bulletin? You have no idea how much work it takes to find a source!" she yelled back. "Getting stuff like that still makes good money."

"I don't care about money! I want to find real treasure!"

I hung up on her with a huff. Ellora was in it for the money, but I was in it for the adventure. And the money was nice, too.

Trotting along the road, I kept an eye out for anything a collector might want. After decades of disrepair shingles were scattered about, long ago blown off roofs. Spindly weeds poked out of the ground. The town was awash in faded paint, cracked wood, and everything else that came from enduring the weather.

Focused on my goal, I made my way to the research lab on the edge of the town. It sat next to the hospital. Both were old-style buildings with short, arched windows and symmetrical portions of the building that stuck out, shaped like halves of hexagons. The lab was three stories and the hospital had one more than that.

I had never stepped into the lab. The thought of what I might find there repelled me, keeping me several yards from the building at all times, as if an invisible bubble blocked it off. The hospital had items that would satisfy Ellora with less chance of running into some sort of horror.

I rushed through the hospital, picking out trinkets here and there that caught my eye. *No one lives here anymore so it's not stealing, right?* I kept a fast pace until I heard a long squeal and froze. Only my ears stirred as I listened for anything that would indicate I wasn't alone.

Nothing came, but I scampered back to the open streets anyway.

Outside, I took a deep breath and repeated what Ellora said in my mind. *It's abandoned. It's abandoned....* I raced back towards the sewer until a rotted sign caught my eye and caused me to slow to a stop.

Fresh pastries. Not so fresh anymore, but it still gave me an idea. I made my way out of the city, eager to meet up with my ride home.

2

Back home, I stopped by a grocer to grab my dad's favorite flavor of berry balls. They weren't actually berries. The illustration of a forgbug on the package showed where they came from. With six legs in front, the bugs stored food in a thin sac that they dragged behind them. The sac could be plucked off without killing the bug. Flavors varied based on what they ate. Farmers fed them different types of berries and protected them so that they could get big, fat sacs.

I liked to call them butt balls to bug Dad. He loved them.

Stuffing them into a cooling unit, I packed it into a box I had been putting together for him. Now that I was getting money I could afford to buy stuff for him, things he'd mentioned being out of. It just needed one more thing.

I flew down the stairs to my dad's room in the basement. Pulling open one of his drawers, I rummaged through our little pile of video sticks stuffed in the back next to his marriage tassel. I'd never seen him wear it – he got divorced shortly after I was born – but it was a white one.

When I grabbed a stick and turned around the image of his empty room struck me. Fixed in place, I stared at it feeling like something was wrong.

Something IS wrong. Dad's not here.

I squeezed the stick in my hand and looked

down. He hadn't come home for my eighteenth birthday. Soon I'd be nineteen. About a year had passed since I'd seen him in person; I could hardly believe it.

My heart ached. The need to talk to him tore through me so badly it hurt. After forcing myself away from his room and back upstairs, I set the stick down and sat in front of the v-phone. I stared at it and took a deep breath before making the call.

He picked up quickly with a smile on the other end. "Leander! Usually I have to call you."

"Yeah." I forced a smile.

"What's going on?"

I shrugged slightly. "Nothing." I took another breath. I'd called him but I didn't have anything to talk about.

His smile faded. "What's wrong?"

Mentally I scolded myself. *It's been a year. It's stupid to get upset about it now.* I couldn't tell him I was upset because he was gone so I picked another topic that had been troubling me.

"It's just school," my voice quivered.

"What happened?"

"The teacher doesn't like the essay I turned in." I became more irritable as I thought about it, muttering the last part, "Even though what I wrote is true."

"Hnn. What did you write about?"

I stiffened. I hadn't thought it through and it wasn't something I wanted to tell my dad about. When I answered I tried to make it as vague as possible,

"About why the Geuranians attacked Nagdecht."

I scrutinized his reaction. He lowered his eyebrows and tilted his head, hesitating to respond.

"What did you say in it?"

I bit my lip, glancing away. "Just ... about stuff that led up to it ..." I tried to be firmer, "But it was all true! She shouldn't flunk me for it!"

He hummed lowly as he mulled it over, nodding twice. "Why don't you send it to me?"

My eyes widened in pure, concentrated horror. I did *not* want my dad to see my essay. My zealous father who was pro-Naggian everything. I already knew he was going to hate it.

"Ah ..." I bumbled around for an excuse but found none. *Maybe I can burn down the house and say it was lost in the fire.*

"Send me a copy of the file. I'll let you know what I think."

That's exactly what I feared. Without an excuse to fall back on, I had to answer. "All right."

He gave me a reassuring smile. "Cheer up. We'll figure it out."

I tried to smile as if that didn't terrify me.

"So what else have you been up to?"

We had a short chat. He talked about what they were doing at the camp; I mentioned a few things about school. Soon our conversation came to an end and he went back to work.

I printed out a picture of me and him and finished putting together my package. Before heading out to mail it, I took care of some household tasks without issue until I carried the kitchen scraps outside to put in our small compost heap. Upon going outside I spotted a lympet in the corner of the garden, digging. Small and scraggly, it had short stumpy legs, a round face with giant ears and a fluffy tail.

The deceptively cute critters were the scourge of gardens everywhere. They ate roots and insects, which spelled doom for a defenseless garden. I snatched up the hose and sprayed water at it, shouting at it as it scurried away through the front fence, "Get out of here! Go dig up someone else's garden!"

The last thing I wanted when Dad finally came home was for the yard to be a mess of withered plants. Like most in the city we had a small backyard with enough room for some shrubs and a single tree – ours had a branch that bent sharply towards the earth. Some idiot snapped it while trying to climb on it as a kid and then tried to hide it from his dad, and it ended up healing that way.

After fixing the fruit plant that had been half dug up, I set off to mail the package and then to my next goal: Ellora. I still had some words for her. That meant seeing Galloughs, though.

Galloughs and I clashed before I even knew who he was. Had more time passed before we met again we may not have remembered each other, but shortly after I agreed to work with Ellora she set him up as a way for me to contact her, and when I walked to the bar I recognized it well. He never had any faith in my abilities, constantly tried to discourage me from getting involved with the black market and didn't take me seriously at all. I wouldn't let him stop me, though. Treasure hunting was what I wanted to do.

My dad worked on the v-phone my entire life with no chance of promotion or raise. The only benefit was the ability to work from home. He dreamed of being a soldier, and he was, but he was stuck in the same dead-end job for 17 years. I appreciated what he did but I didn't want to end up like that. *I won't put off my dreams and no one will convince me otherwise.* That thought pulled me through the year while Ellora sent me off to do odd jobs, but my resolve was wearing thin.

I shoved the door to the bar open and stepped in. My presence made no impact. In the afternoon, only a few stragglers wandered in. Galloughs manned the counter, keeping it impeccably clean, as usual.

I braced myself for the coming conversation and approached. He watched in silence. Putting on a cool air, I rested an elbow on the counter and leaned forward. "I need to talk to Ellora."

"You seem to be in a bad mood," he remarked. *He's just waiting for me to say something he can use against me.*

"I'm fine. Ellora just needs to do a better job finding information."

"The market is a dirty business, Son. It revolves around money, not flights of fancy."

I pursed my lips. "I know that."

"Then don't complain about how things work." He began to lean towards me but wrinkled his nose. "You stink."

"Yeah, I haven't gotten to take a bath yet," I complained and held up a threatening finger. "Either get Ellora here or I start touching things and show you just how dirty this business is."

He held an arm in front of the glasses. "Keep your filthy hands off my stuff." He pointed towards the side door. "In the back!" he ordered.

I went to a back room. The plain rooms only seemed to exist for meetings like this.

Plopping down on a seat, I leaned back and waited. A year. A whole year. Since I found the flute, Ellora hadn't given me information on anything that could be considered an artifact. *Maybe she never will.* My fingers drummed on the desk as I mentally prepared myself for the confrontation. Face to face she twisted things around on me all the time.

Time dragged until I heard the click of her footsteps down the hall. One of my ears saluted before I turned to face the door.

"Have anything good?" she asked the second she stepped through the door. I cursed her ability to get the first word in.

My eyes turned to my bag. I poured the contents out on the table: the piece of crystal, rusty forceps and some miscellaneous supplies from the hospital. They were old enough for anyone to tell they weren't from a modern day hospital, but common enough to be recognizable.

She eyed them, picking up the crystal.

"It's from a musical tree," I explained.

She shrugged. "I guess this'll do." *The great*

thanks I get.

"I don't want to go back there," I spat it out.

"Oh, stop being such a baby." She brushed me off as she swiped it all into her bag.

"These aren't artifacts!"

"They're old things."

"If you're not going to find anything but scraps then I'm out of here." I slammed my hand on the table and stomped towards the door.

"I guess you're not interested in the king's necklace then," she answered without looking my way.

I stopped.

"The king's necklace?" I repeated with hesitant enthusiasm.

"Do you remember the necklace the previous king wore when he was enthroned?"

I nodded despite not having any recollection of it. Before I realized it I had been lured back into the room.

"It disappeared shortly after he became king. Popular theory is that it was stolen because he replaced the Wind Queen's other son, but that doesn't matter."

I twitched an ear. The first son's rule had been so short that history teachers used it as a trick question. "Who ruled after Queen Lambrian?" Students usually answered "King Lariat," completely forgetting the first son.

"What matters is that it's been found."

I blinked. "So someone else found it? Where is it?"

"Up north. Some of the people who make black market goods have it."

I stared at her, confused. "But didn't you say before not to undermine people?"

"*Our* people. I don't care about their people."

Sneaking into an unguarded place like Wilten Crags, while it had its challenges, was a lot different than stealing from black marketers who would be highly protective of their prize.

"How am I supposed to get it?" I asked.

"That's the best part. The woman who ran their gang died, and it split into two groups. All you have to do is sneak in unnoticed, take it, and they'll blame each other," she spoke with a smirk.

I nodded. It made sense but it sounded risky.

"I'll have to come up with some sort of excuse to travel up there." I looked to the ground as if it would have answers.

"I have that covered, too," she replied instantly. "One of the dancers at the theater is going up there for surgery. I said I could send someone along to help him out."

It sounded like Ellora really did have it all planned out. I'd underestimated her.

Thoughts of finding a brand new treasure raced through my mind and a smile found its way to my lips before I knew it.

"All right, tell me everything you know."

3

When I arrived at the edge of the city I searched the station for someone injured or sickly but I didn't see anyone. Other people flocked under the lights as we all waited for our ride north. Secretly, I hoped for a hovercraft. They zoomed along at speeds of 500 or 600 miles per hour compared to other vehicles which reached top speeds of a few hundred.

As I meandered, my eye caught a young man inching my way. When our eyes met he hesitated, but came closer again.

"Are you Leander?"

I looked him over. Fit and healthy, with a lean body. Something about him looked familiar but I couldn't place it.

"Yeah. You're Ellora's friend?"

"Yes, I'm a dancer at the theater." A smile crept onto his face as he held out a hand. "I'm Valli."

A dancer? I think I've seen her with a dancer before. I took his hand. His skin was soft and his grip gentle.

A moment later, the truck arrived. No hovercraft for me, but I should have expected that.

Essentially a string of beds on wheels, two carts were hitched to the back of the truck. Before we had a chance to get further acquainted, attendants led us to our spots. I let Valli have the bottom bed even though he seemed to be capable of climbing.

I found myself lying on top of the plain white sheets and staring at the bunk above mine as we rumbled along. My racing mind kept me awake far longer than I wanted. I didn't know what to expect of Valli or this place.

Finally sleep hunted me down. When I woke up, people were being ushered out of the truck and shuffling to different intersections to board carts. I grabbed our bags and walked to the one that looked the least crowded. The morning air had a bigger bite to it than I was used to at home, and I was thankful I remembered to pack the warmest coats and jackets I had. We picked the closest dining cart. I didn't care what type of food it was, so long as we got breakfast. There, Valli and I settled across from each other at a table.

I glanced across at the perfect stranger. He kept a pleasant smile on his face and I tried to return it. His hair hung to his waist with a ribbon flower pinned to it -- aptly named for the overly long sepals that hung down like ribbons.

Nagdecht had two ideals when it came to looks. One was like the generals -- large, tall, strong, with wide shoulders and imposing figures. The other was like the king -- more modest in height with softer, more delicate features and leaner bodies. Men and women often strove to be one of the two. Valli was the latter. That someone from the theater was beautiful shouldn't have surprised me. A theater as famous as the Wind Queen's probably had thousands of applicants to pick from.

Besides being Ellora's friend, I knew next to nothing about him.

"So ... You're getting surgery?" I asked with a piece of my breakfast dangling from my fork.

He nodded. "I'm pretty excited about it."

I smiled. *Is it too forward to ask what it's for?* I couldn't see any reason for it. He didn't look sick or hurt in any way. Curiosity ate at me but asking outright felt too awkward, so I tried a different route.

"What's your score? I'm an 11.2." I pointed to my ears. "Hearing problems on my mom's side."

The Genetics, Intelligence, Charisma and Health test. It measured how desirable a person's genes were on a 15 point scale, where 15 was perfect and someone with a 1 was probably dead. Most averaged from 9 to 12.5. All Naggians knew their score and knew why they had their score. Mine was much lower than my dad's. He had me tested when I was younger to try and raise my score, but it turned out I was a carrier for the hearing loss gene and my score didn't budge.

"I'm a 13.1," he answered with that ever-present smile.

Above average. It couldn't be a genetic problem with a score like that.

"So ..." I made a circle in the air with my hand. "Why exactly are you ...?"

His smile dropped momentarily as he focused on me and I inwardly shrank, but it almost immediately popped back on before he responded, "Oh, it's elective."

"Really? What for?" The words made their way

out of my mouth before they even reached my brain.

"Just a little chest surgery."

My eyes dropped to his chest. I couldn't help it; they did it without my permission. "You look fine to me."

His expression looked tense despite the smile. "Thank you. But I'm still getting the surgery."

I nodded and dropped the subject. "Sorry, I don't mean to pry."

"It's all right."

We stared. I took another bite, looking for something to fill the silence.

"So how did you end up at the theater?"

"I've trained as a dancer since I was little. I always loved it. When I graduated I started out at a circus, with magic shows and acrobatics." His smile broadened as he leaned forward. "I even learned a little magic. Want to see?"

"Sure."

He pulled out a neatly folded rag and held it up. "Okay, I'm going to make this disappear."

I rested my arms on the table, eyes fixed on him.

"Keep your eye on it," he told me as he brought up his second hand to cover it. "Don't look away. Keeping looking, and ..."

He tossed it over his shoulder in plain sight, then held up his empty hands. "Ta-da!"

I raised my eyebrows before letting out an amused huff.

"Now for my next trick ..." he let the sentence fade off as he covered his mouth with a hand and giggled at his own joke. Seconds later he picked up the cloth, fussing about litter.

I leaned back and relaxed. He was nothing like Ellora, that was for sure.

When we arrived at the hotel, I slung my suitcase to the side. The room had two beds and standard furnishings. I plopped down in front of the desk. First things first, I needed to call my dad. I didn't want him to think I was missing.

He answered, but when the video popped up he was glancing down with a quizzical expression.

"Hi, Dad," I started cheerfully.

"Hi." He hesitated before looking up. "This says you're in Woodlor."

Why did he have to notice little details like that? I froze momentarily as I came up with an explanation.

"Oh, well ..." I stammered, "I came here to help a friend."

"A friend?"

"Yeah ..." I glanced over at Valli sitting on the edge of the bed. He caught my look and came over to the desk.

"This is your father?" he asked, leaning down to be in view.

"Yeah. This is Valli," I introduced him.

"Hello." Valli waved.

I could see cynicism on my dad's face. He'd never met this person before; I'd only known him for a little while myself. But Dad was polite when he replied, "Good morning."

Valli explained in an upbeat tone, "It's a pleasure meeting you. I came here for an operation and Leander volunteered to help while I was healing. I should thank you for letting me borrow him."

My dad nodded, acknowledging him. "I see. Well, if it's for a friend ..."

Valli backed away to finish unpacking.

"You didn't tell me you were going there."

"I wasn't exactly planning on it. It sort of came up last minute."

"Hmm. What about your school work?"

"I brought my paper with me," I assured him.

He nodded again, accepting the excuses. "Don't forget to take care of that." *Ever vigilant about my education.*

"I won't."

"Is anything else going on over there?"

"No, I was just calling to check in."

"Well, I'm glad you checked in, but I don't have much time this morning." The corners of his mouth edged up slightly. "Oh, one more thing."

He bent over and picked something up off-screen.

I flicked one ear, focusing on the video. "Hmm?"

He held up the picture I sent him and placed it in view with one finger pointing towards my face. "What sort of expression is this?"

He got it. My heart soared and I laughed.

In the picture he and I were wrestling in a pool when I was about twelve. He had both arms around me and I was glaring up at him with a devious grin on my face, ready to take him down.

That wouldn't work out for me, though. Even now I couldn't beat my dad wrestling. It wasn't fair; he was taller, fitter, and had military training.

"It looks like you're plotting." He turned the picture towards himself.

"I *was* plotting," I allowed a moment of silence before adding in a menacing voice, "revenge."

He chuckled. "All right, then. I love you."

I glanced to the side where Valli was sitting and hid my face behind my hand, mumbling, "I love you, too."

"Take care."

He shut off the feed.

"You two sound close," Valli commented from his bed.

"We've always been close."

"That's good." He grinned. "With your mom, too?"

I furrowed my brows. "No, not really."

"Oh?"

"I never really knew her and I don't really want to," I answered as I walked over to my bed to sit down and sort my things. I met my mother a few times. More often I thought I would meet her and she wouldn't show up. I'd decided long ago that if she didn't want to see me then I didn't want to see her. Dad was there for everything I needed anyway. I didn't need her.

"That's too bad." He ducked his head down to focus on his luggage.

I shrugged. Nothing new to me.

"You can borrow one of mine," he offered.

Two moms? So he was probably adopted.

"I'll stick with my dad, thanks."

After we unpacked our necessities he spoke up with a shaky voice, "I suppose I should go to the hospital and let them know I'm here."

"Something wrong?"

"I'm just nervous." He brushed his hair back with his hand, hiding part of his face.

"But I thought you were getting this because you wanted it?"

"Yes, but … I'm still a little scared something could go wrong. I need to be in good shape to be able to dance."

"I'm sure you'll be fine in time for the next show."

He shook his head. "I won't be in the next one. I helped with the writing instead."

"The writing? Aren't they already written?" I leaned on the edge of the bed, looking back at him.

"We're doing a play based off of a book, so we had to re-write it for the theater."

"Oh, really? What book?"

"It's called *The Prisoner*."

"I think I've heard of that somewhere before."

"It's about a Geuranian guard who falls in love

with a Naggian prisoner, and they end up running off together. Very controversial. People have been making a ruckus about us doing a play about it, but that's how we stay in the news. People wouldn't talk about us if we did standard shows." He glanced around the room before whispering, "Want to see something neat?"

I turned on the bed to face him all the way. "What is it?"

He dug through his bag again, taking out a pair of necklaces and holding them out. "These are genuine Geuranian goods."

"Oh?" I leaned forward to take a closer look. They had a different style with sharp edges and straight lines rather than the curves and natural shapes worn around Nagdecht, but nothing seemed that special about them.

"Some people don't think we should buy anything from Geuran, but the theater likes to be authentic. It's neat to get to see things Geuranians actually used, isn't it?" he spoke quicker than normal with a glimmer in his eye. "They let me bring them since they know I like them."

"Oh, yeah ..." I had trouble mimicking his excitement. If I hadn't been to Geuran myself it might have been more interesting, but I'd already seen so much more of the place.

"Ah." He placed a hand over them, expression falling. "I mean ... You're not upset the theater spends money on things like this, are you? I just think it's interesting. We don't usually get to see things like this."

My eyes turned up to meet his. "Oh, no, that's

not it. I don't mind. It's just that," I spun my hand around, trying to explain, "It's just ... Well, I've been there."

I gritted my teeth, gauging his response. His eyes widened and his mouth hung open momentarily.

"You mean to Geuran?"

"Yeah."

"Are you serious?"

"Yeah, about a year ago."

"But how did you even get in? And why? Wasn't it scary?" He covered his mouth, barely finishing each question before spitting out another one.

I rubbed the back of my neck, averting my eyes. I was used to dealing with Ellora, and she didn't tend to be excited or amazed by anything I did.

"It wasn't that bad. It's kind of a long story, but I went there to find something they stole from Nagdecht. It's not quite as bad as you'd think."

"Really?" He was leaning forward so much I thought he might climb over my bed. "What was it like?"

As I told him about the town I first saw and he listened intently to every word I gained confidence, and before I knew it I was telling him about sneaking through military camps and breaking into their storage facility. I made sure to leave out Deckard; even if he was fascinated by Geuran it didn't mean he'd be okay with having Geuranian friends.

I wowed him with my retelling until we needed to go to the hospital. Impressing someone with my story felt nice. As we picked up our things to go, I held my head up a little higher.

From there we went to the hospital. Even though helping Valli was just a cover story I still felt obligated to do it. I waited for him in the lounge and idly flipped through an access panel for anything interesting to read. I found myself continuously piercing the hologram with my finger and watching the menu have tremors as I wiggled it about.

When he stepped out I perked up. We could finally get out of here, and I could go do what I really came here to do.

"How did it go?"

"Fine. They gave me a list of foods they would like me to eat, and I'll have to fast about half a day before surgery."

No more details were discussed beyond the niceties. I escorted him back to the hotel and flew back out like a gust of wind to see if I could check the place Ellora had told me about. Unfortunately, no sooner had I stepped out of the hotel room than Valli was a step behind me.

"You don't have to come." I tried to gently shoo him away.

"It's better than being bored at the hotel all day." He met my pace, folding his hands in front of him. "Where are you going?"

"I'm just looking up stuff."

He followed me and I tried to think of how to leave him behind. The scent of freshly baked bread wafted through the air. He caught my arm and pointed

26

at the bakery.

"That smells delicious. Since you came all the way here to help me how about I treat you? I'd like to eat something while I still can."

It seemed Ellora forgot to tell him why I was really here.

Colorful nut breads and fruit breads sat on display in the window. They looked moist and smelled amazing. The baker clearly had a passion for his or her craft.

Still, I needed to take the opportunity to leave him behind if I could.

"I'm not hungry, but go ahead without me. I can meet up with you back at the hotel later."

He frowned, but stopped at the bakery. I didn't wait. I ran to the nearest access panel and brought up a map, studying it. The place I needed to go was outside of the town. Tons of abandoned warehouses and factories littered the outskirts -- a sign of the times. The noble here had specialized in basic flat-screen technology and people rarely used that anymore. Holograms had long taken its place, especially with publicly used equipment. I wasn't sure how they kept revenue coming in here anymore.

After I memorized the basic layout, I stuck my ID card in the panel and boarded a cart for the edge of the city.

The city ended abruptly. From buildings to dirt. I walked a short distance through a deserted area overtaken by weeds and brush. The abandoned warehouse took about twenty minutes to get to. I hid in some brush in the distance to watch. Several minutes of silence passed.

A rustling from behind caused me to jump and twirl around, only to see Valli holding a basket.

"Leander?" His voice sounded all too loud.

"Shh!" I hushed him as he settled down beside me. "What are you doing here?"

"The line wasn't long so I went after you, but you boarded a cart before I could get there. I saw your destination, though, so I followed you," he explained. "But … what are you doing here?"

"I heard there was some illegal activity so I came to check it out." I managed to get something out but I didn't have a whole explanation formed in my head yet.

He glanced at the warehouse. No one had shown up there yet, but we hadn't been there long.

"Why are you doing that?" he asked, confusion evident in his voice.

"Because … they need to be arrested."

"Do you work with the police?" he sounded doubtful.

"Not exactly. It's complicated, but I can't talk about it." I did my best to stay vague and hope he wouldn't keep asking questions.

He stared at the warehouse in silence. I felt uncomfortable with him there. Not just because he didn't know what was going on, but I didn't want him around if trouble started.

"If there's illegal activity, why don't you just call

the police?"

I spouted out the first excuse that came to my mind, "We have to find evidence first."

Just as he was going to say something else a truck came rumbling from the distance. I held up a hand to hush him, and we watched as the truck pulled up. A person hopped out, opened the large doors, and drove the truck inside. It barely fit through the opening.

At least I know there's activity around here now, but I can't sleuth with Valli here. I'll have to come back later.

"So ..." My eyes fell on the basket. "You bought something?"

He opened the lid, showing off a fruit bread covered in a powdered sugar with blue jam on top. I could feel it dissolving on my tongue already.

"That looks more like a dessert. Maybe we could go have lunch first?" I suggested. *Any reason to get out of here.*

"What about what you're doing here?"

"It's fine, let's go." I led the way back.

Walking back into town I noticed a lot of people out. The bustling morning crowd, which got thicker the farther we went in, surprised me. As we approached a café, too many people were out, chattering excitedly.

When the waiter came to our table I asked her, "What's going on?"

Energy pumped through her as well. She answered with a large grin, "General Glaive was spotted in town. They say he passed by here somewhere."

29

"General Glaive? Why would he be way up here?"

"I don't know. Business, I'd assume." She shrugged. "What would you like to have?"

A few snowflakes drifted down from the sky. There was only one thing to order on a chilly day.

"Clam chowder, please."

It was a family tradition. On cold days Dad and I would make a big pot of clam chowder and take it down to his room. He'd close the door, turn on the heat and we'd hang out there and talk. We had a lot of important conversations on those days: why my GICH score was lower than his, where babies came from, what to do if aliens came and tried to eat us. I'd spend the night in his room -- he said it was better than heating up the whole house.

The capital didn't get cold often, but when it did, those were some of my favorite nights.

When our food came to the table, I paused as soon as the chowder hit my mouth. Ever since my dad left I hadn't been able to find any place in the capital that made it the way he did, but the chowder here tasted just like his. It was perfect. The clams were smaller but more abundant and the seasoning had just the right amount of punch in it. Nostalgia warmed me.

A glimpse of a white and red jacket snapped me back to reality. *General Glaive?* Not many soldiers would be this far north. Like everyone else, I leaned over to get a look.

It wasn't General Glaive but he was oddly familiar. He had a short cut, slicked back with some thin bangs on one side. His face was long with eyes that sloped downward.

"He looks familiar," I murmured to Valli. His eyes turned the direction mine did and widened.

"One of the Melechtion."

Then I recognized him. "Glaive's men". People called them the Melechtion Group because Glaive granted them all the noble name Melechtion, after a man who, in history, was recognized for his outstanding loyalty to the queen.

He started out with three men, and recently a fifth had joined. They were famous for holding the highest position anyone could achieve in the army, save for general. They were also well-known because the position didn't exist before Glaive became the general.

"I wonder what they're doing here," I whispered.

"I don't know," Valli responded in awe as he continued to stare. I didn't worry about attracting their attention when dozens of other people were looking. I spotted another soldier walking with him. I recognized the second one more quickly.

"That's Tyrus."

The newest Melechtion. I knew his face well. He had his hair cut to the shoulder like I did, as long as the army allowed. Of all the Melechtion, he stuck out the most, the problem being that it was for all the wrong reasons. His GICH score was 11.1. *Lower* than mine. Fine for the average citizen, but for the general's elite it didn't add up. All the others had scores above 14. On top of that, he was short, only an inch taller than me. Again, average, whereas his colleague was several inches taller.

Nothing about him screamed, "elite." I didn't know if I should be confused or inspired. After all, if he could make it to the top, maybe I could, too. He was a lot like me, down to the thin, angular face.

"Dorrius," Valli murmured the name of the other soldier. He was considered number one of the men, even though Glaive hired the first three at the same time.

As they walked by, I strained my ear to listen to them. Valli did the same across the table. I managed to catch a few odd words over the chatter.

Dorrius spoke in a calm tone, "… after we see the police … a meeting later …"

While Dorrius focused on Tyrus, Tyrus's eyes continuously meandered, noticing the crowd of people staring at them. I only caught a single word he said, "… castle …"

Dorrius continued speaking without acknowledging the watchers, his voice clear, "… you're … around here … visiting?"

Though I couldn't hear Tyrus' response, his expression tensed, a frown creasing his face. After that they were out of hearing range.

We both strained to see them through the crowd when a cart lowered in front of them and they vanished inside. I never thought of myself as the starstruck type but it was hard not to look.

"Dorrius is handsome." Valli sighed.

I cocked a brow at him with a smirk. "Are you planning on seducing him?"

He laughed. "I doubt someone like me could get one of them."

"Why not? You're pretty enough." It flowed out easily from me, like stating a fact.

His brows drew together, mouth forming a straight line. "You really think so?"

"Sure." I shrugged.

He relaxed again with a soft smile, and we went back to our meals, chatting. I told him how I'd wanted to come in a hovercraft. He told me about how neither of his parents could dance at all, and we wasted the time until we went back to the hotel. I made a mental note to order the chowder again before I left the city.

4

The next morning I escorted Valli back to the hospital. I bounced at the reception desk until a nurse came and got him, then went back to the hotel to grab some supplies, ready to head out. First, I needed to check in with Dad so he wouldn't worry about me.

As soon as his image popped up, I began with a cheerful, "Hi!" eager to keep the conversation brief.

"You seem happy today."

"Just looking forward to stuff." I stayed vague.

"I read your essay."

My heart stopped. I was so distracted by my mission that I forgot about my essay. At that moment, I must have looked like a small animal going face to face with a predator.

"I'm not sure where you got all of these ideas from. They were definitely ... interesting." He rested his cheek on his palm. My stomach clenched, but I prepared to defend my position.

"I was a little surprised you mentioned the famine we had over a decade ago."

"But we attacked them back then," I clarified.

"That wasn't a declaration of war, though. We were in a state of emergency."

"That's not how they would see it." I tried to maintain an even tone.

"I can give you that, but I have to disagree with

the part about the army. We do have more people total, but only about 10% of our population is in the army, while their entire male population joins the army, so our armies are about the same size."

He had a point; our army didn't outnumber theirs like Deckard had said. I wasn't ready to concede that, though. "But the way they see it we could easily double or triple the size of our army and they can't."

"It's not likely that many people will join the army. Our government is set up differently than theirs. People aren't forced to join."

"We might feel that way but *they* don't." I felt my argument slipping away.

"Even if those things are true, it doesn't excuse them from invading our country." He shook his head.

"They were afraid of us," I desperately explained. "We already attacked them before when they didn't provoke us, and we have more people. They were afraid of what would happen if we had technology they couldn't compete with."

Dad sighed and folded his arms, leaning back in his chair. "Do you understand what the problem is with your essay?"

I stared quietly at him, awaiting the explanation.

"Leander ..." his voice softened. "If you had been killed in that attack I would be horribly offended by this. You can't excuse what they did. Hundreds of innocent people died."

"But it's true!"

"Even if everything you said is true, I wish you

would think about the big picture." He leaned forward, folding his hands. "Your teacher is the only one who is ever going to see it and she's not interested in listening to it. What will you accomplish with this besides making yourself miserable?"

My heart sank. I couldn't think of anything it would accomplish.

He took a breath and continued, "Rewrite your paper. If you really believe this you'll have opportunities to make a difference later. You have to pick your battles."

"But I shouldn't get a bad grade just for writing a different point of view--"

"It's not bad that you want to try and understand them, but you still have to be sensitive to people here. There's no justifying what happened." He kept firm.

My face fell as I looked away. I didn't want to offend anyone. I just wanted to tell the truth.

"Maybe you could be an ambassador in the future," he softened.

I figured he was trying to cheer me up but I went for it anyway, looking back up. "Do you really think that could happen?"

"I don't know." He shrugged. "Maybe not in my lifetime, but anything could happen."

If Geuran and Nagdecht got along, I could talk to Deckard again. Was he still puttering around the northern part of the border? Still getting in trouble?

"Leander ..." he spoke gently, "I should get going."

"Nn." I stared down at the desk the v-phone was sitting on.

"I love you."

"Yeah ..." I was too upset to say it back.

He waited expectantly for a moment before saying, "I'll talk to you later."

The feed ended. It was as hard as I thought it would be. My dad tore my paper apart. I just wanted Naggians to understand Geuranians a little, but Naggians weren't interested in hearing it.

I shoved myself away from the table, letting the chair roll back. I'd lost my energy but I still had a mission to complete. I picked up my bag, making my way down to the lobby with a grim face.

When I swung the door open to go out I nearly bumped into Valli.

I stumbled back, startled. "What are you doing here?"

He looked disappointed, shaking his head with a sigh. "I'll have to wait until tomorrow for the surgery." He looked me over and his pitch became higher, "Where are you going?"

He took me off guard again. When he surprised me I'd completely forgotten what I was doing.

"Oh, just ... Going to do some stuff real fast." I fumbled for the words.

"Can I come with you?"

"You should probably stay here and get some rest." I did my best to discourage him.

"But it's so boring sitting around waiting," he

groaned. "I want to do something."

Frustration built up in me. I needed to get to the warehouse, but I couldn't have Valli tagging along with me everywhere. If I had nothing else to do I wouldn't have minded his company, but he didn't need to be put in any danger.

No, I'm the one being weird. He just wants to do normal stuff, I told myself.

I calmed myself down and smiled. "I guess we could go shopping or something." His variety of fancy dresses suggested he might enjoy it.

"That sounds great!" he readily agreed, and in what felt like seconds, he'd dragged me to a nearby store where we browsed for clothes. At least he did. I followed a step behind him as he looked through various dresses. Even if I wore dresses, they all looked too expensive for me.

He turned to me, holding one up in front of himself. "What do you think?"

The soft purple fabric glistened in the light, with a pattern of pink flowers at the bottom.

"It suits you," I admitted.

"Aren't you going to look for something?"

I gave him a blank look, unsure what to say without offending him. Nothing here looked like something I would wear. I was the type who got dirty and ripped my things.

"Just kidding." He chuckled. "This doesn't look like it's quite your style."

A sigh of relief escaped my lips.

"Thanks for coming with me. I'd rather not go around town by myself."

"No problem." I grinned at him. "You're easier to get along with than Ellora."

I worried that he might get upset, but he smiled weakly. "She can be a little pushy." Then he covered his mouth. "Don't tell her I said that."

"I won't." I had stronger words for her. "Why are you friends with her, anyway? You're a lot nicer than she is."

"I think it's impressive how far she's gotten, especially considering both her parents are in jail."

I cocked a brow at him. "They're in jail?"

"Oh." He stopped, wide-eyed. "I thought you knew. I guess I shouldn't have said anything."

Ellora and I kept things to business. I wasn't sure what to say. Whether or not I liked her, I couldn't deny she had a successful career and was ambitious.

"I won't tell her," I assured him. "I guess you're right that she's successful."

"I'm a little jealous of her, honestly," his voice shrank.

"What? Why?"

"I've been at the theater longer than her, but she's a lot more popular than I am. I guess that's just the way it is. She's a singer and I'm a backup dancer." He tilted his head. "I don't like to be in the spotlight but I want attention. It doesn't make much sense, does it?"

"I get it. A lot of people dream about being famous but don't really want to be."

"She's also nice to have around in arguments. I've never been very good with confrontations." He shrugged a shoulder and wrinkled his nose with a grin. I thought back to when Ellora told me she would kill me if anything happened to him. She probably did handle the confrontations for him.

I glanced down at the dress folded and draped over his arm. "So are we done here, then?"

He nodded. "I don't have much space to bring back a lot of stuff."

"Then you can go ahead and go back. I have some things I need to get to."

He seemed reluctant to part ways but I didn't wait to convince him. If I kept putting it off, I'd never get anything done. I left the store while he was still checking out and hopped on the nearest cart to the edge of the city. This time I knew where to go to get to the warehouse.

As I knelt down and watched, I was disappointed. The only windows were placed high on the building, far out of reach, and I couldn't see through them.

A rustling caught my ear and I ducked farther into the brush, hooking my sleeve on a branch. My fear faded as Valli came into view.

"How did you know I was here?" I whispered harshly.

"It's where you went yesterday, right?" He settled behind the brush with me. "What are you doing, anyway?"

"Just ... It's private business, okay?"

I didn't know what else to tell him. I wasn't much of a liar and I didn't feel like I could tell him the truth. If Ellora didn't explain it to him, I didn't want to tell him.

"Leander ..." He looked at me with a worried expression.

"Yeah?" I spat it out even though I felt bad about it.

His eyes turned down for a second before he answered, brows furrowed, "Never mind."

At this rate, I'd never get anything done.

"Look, just stay here, okay? I have something I need to do," I told him, holding up my hands, "Just. Stay. Here."

I crept towards the warehouse, glancing back to make sure Valli didn't follow. I couldn't walk through the door, though; people might be inside. Sneaking to the back, I looked up at a small window. Too high to reach.

I searched for anything to stand on. The warehouse had weeds and dry grass growing around it and not much else. On the side I found an old water heater. The box that enclosed it was rusted shut and dented. If I stood on top, I could probably reach the roof.

With a push I gauged how sturdy it was. *Too bad it's not a box. They're always reliable allies.*

I pulled myself on top; waves of adrenaline washed through me when it wobbled. I ignored the movement and kept climbing. It creaked when I stood up and I threw my hands up to grab the edge of the roof. Using every muscle in my body, I heaved myself up and rolled onto the roof. That done, I ran to the back of the building.

Even though I could reach the window with my foot I didn't want to enter it without seeing what was on the other side. Which meant I had tricky maneuvering to do. I hung off the building and stretched out my hand until I got a grip on the window sill. Taking in a breath, I let myself drop. I struggled to hang onto the window. My second hand caught the other side. My arms hurt from the strain, but I managed to drag myself up and glance in the window.

Boxes were stacked close to the ceiling on the other side. My old friends. I could hear some indistinct chattering.

My feet scrambled against the wall to push myself up. The window was tiny – definitely not meant for people to be climbing into, but I squeezed through it. One hand grabbed the top of the boxes as I forced my body through, using it and the sill for support until I dropped to the ground.

The thump I made when I hit the ground paralyzed me. I listened to the voices to see if anyone heard me. The chattering stayed the same. I could hear mentions of "goods" and something about getting them first, but nothing that interested me. I had a necklace to find.

The boxes wrapped around the sides and back of the room, stacked well above my head, leaving a narrow passage for me between the crates and walls. I couldn't see anything on the other side. They reminded me of the large ammunition crates I'd hidden inside of in Geuran. *It's not likely someone would hide a necklace in one of these. Something like that would probably be kept on someone's person or in a secured place.*

The stack came to an end several feet from the front wall. From there, I peeked out to see three people in the middle of the room. Two women and a man. They had grown silent, so I moved with greater care. In the opposite corner, I saw the door of the warehouse. The rest of the front was taken up by a giant garage door.

One woman sat on a box with her elbow on one of her legs and her cheek resting on the palm of her hand. She stared at the garage door, tapping her foot, as the man paced and the other woman stood in place with her arms folded.

More importantly, pistols hung at their waists. I ducked farther behind the boxes. *I need to figure out where to look without attracting attention.* Nothing I'd seen yet caught my eye. They probably had other places like this. If I could get more information I might be able to figure out where it was, but they weren't chatting anymore.

I narrowed my eyes as I glanced around the box again. The man had stopped pacing to look at the floor, shifting his feet. The scraping of his shoes produced the only sound in the whole place.

A powerful thump on the door broke the silence, echoing across the warehouse. We all jumped, attention on the door. I crouched lower. Another thump. Something large was slamming into the door.

My eyes darted to the three people in the middle of the room as the one who was sitting hopped to her feet and took out her gun. The other two took steps back.

The man muttered something between gritted teeth, and I barely caught the last words, "Let's get out of here." Another thump.

The woman with her gun out scolded him, "There's just one of her and three of us. Come on!"

My fingers touched the floor as I got ready to flee, but my eyes stayed glued to the door.

At the woman's prompting the other two fumbled with their guns. The door trembled with the next pounding. Three bangs pierced the air when the second woman fired in the direction of the noise. I winced and covered my ears. Everything stopped. I heard the heavy breathing of the people in the room and saw them still staring at the door, but I couldn't tell if the bullets had gone through.

My own breathing quickened as I stood paralyzed. Time crawled along.

Then, with a crack, the edge of something rounded and sharp sliced through the door, only to be pulled back. More bullets flew, but it cut through the door again. This time I could see the weapon better.

An *axe*. From the looks of it, an iron or steel double-edged battle axe. I'd only ever seen such things in storybooks.

A foot smashed through the destroyed door and knocked the bottom half off its hinge. The upper half twisted and came undone. The enormous woman holding the axe stepped over the threshold into the room. She was covered in a thick, padded armor. It looked bulky and heavy, but with her massive height and muscular body, the extra weight seemed like nothing to her. A gun was strapped to her waist, but the large axe felt more imposing. As if that weren't enough, she had a helmet with two horns curled around her ears on either side. She looked straight out of some fantasy novel.

I inched backwards for more cover. No one was concerned about finding me, though. With all the noise, I doubted they would hear me even if I jumped up and down.

She closed in on the three. Two scampered towards the back while the first woman emptied her pistol. The bullets may have hit the woman with the axe, but they didn't stop her. In mere seconds, the woman with the gun ducked.

She caught herself with a hand to keep from toppling over. On the swing back, she went even lower, flattening all the way to the ground as the axe flew by and hit the crate she'd been using as a seat. The crate hurled through the air and landed several feet away, smashing with a thunderous noise and sliding to a stop. All as if it was nothing more than kicking a ball to this juggernaut.

The woman scrambled to her feet, reaching for the easiest thing she could grab. Her hand gripped one of the horns and yanked on it, but the horn came off as if it had been held on with nothing more than tape. She stumbled back because of her own momentum and dropped the horn.

The woman rolled away. Then the axe came down. I flinched.

The tips of blades struck the ground on either side of the woman's neck, pinning her between them. In a flurry, the other woman and man stopped yards away with guns drawn. All movement stopped at once. The woman on the floor had nowhere to move. The two on the side stood frozen with their guns pointed. Did they even have bullets left? The giant put a foot on the other side of one of the axe blades, holding it firmly in place. The only sound was heavy breathing.

"You guys think you're real clever, trying to grab our stash," the axe-wielder spoke in a deep tone. "The Scraper has a message for you. Tell Lieran that the Mosley is *our* territory, and he better not forget it."

Silence swept the room. No one stirred from their spot for several seconds. The corner of her lip twitched up as she looked at the other two.

The man, hands shaking, asked, "What?"

"I only need one of you to tell him."

The axe came up and I ducked completely behind the boxes, covering my eyes. It slammed against the floor with a clang. More shouting, screaming, two gunshots and I heard them trample over the door. I peeked out just in time to see them being chased out. I hesitated for a minute before I edged out from behind the boxes. My eyes scanned the room until I confirmed there weren't any bodies on the floor.

Are they going to make it? My heart slammed against my chest looking for an escape. If I wasn't smart enough to get out of here it didn't intend to wait for me.

This wasn't worth it. No matter how valuable the necklace was, this wasn't worth it at all. I didn't care what Ellora would say; I was going home. All I needed to do was get out of here without being spotted.

I knew one thing for sure: I wasn't walking out through the door. I needed to act while they were all distracted. For the first time, I walked out into the open and surveyed the room. Crates, crates everywhere. They must have been the 'stash' she was talking about. I could reach the window from on top of them.

I climbed the boxes like a staircase and headed back to the window. At the back, I sat down on the edge of a crate and reached below to grab the window, slipping off and dragging myself up with numb arms. While I struggled to get through, I spotted two trucks outside. *More of them?*

Shoving myself out of the window, I fell back to the floor. I didn't want anyone to see me sticking out. During my trek back, a noise at the door brought me to a full stop. I perked my ears up. One set of heavy footsteps. They lumbered into the warehouse, coming to a stop somewhere in the middle. Something scraped across the floor then fell silent.

Taking my time to pad around the room without making a sound, I looked for a spot to peek out. I didn't want to poke my head around a corner – not this time. A tiny crack between two crates served as a peephole.

In the middle of the floor, seated on the same crate as the previous woman had, the axe wielder wiped her axe with a cloth. I tried not to think about what she was cleaning off. After a minute she bent down to pick up her horn and snapped it back onto the helmet.

I was stuck. I could only hope she would leave without noticing me.

A moment later the garage door opened with a hum and the two trucks pulled into the building. The woman stood, hooking her axe to her back. When the trucks rumbled to a stop the drivers got out – one woman, one man. The woman was short and petite, the man slightly larger than her.

"I told you she'd have the place cleared out by the time we got here," the woman told him as they congregated in the middle.

"I still don't like the odds. There's a lot more of them than us." His voice was more anxious.

"Didn't make much of a difference here, did it?" she jested. Her hand rested on the other woman's arm as she shot her a grin. It made the larger woman hesitate before pulling away, suddenly subdued instead of domineering.

"Just get the trucks loaded." The giant walked by them, lifting one of the heavy crates by herself. The newcomers each took one side of a crate and carried it together.

"Did you get hurt at all?" the smaller woman asked. The ponytail she wore high on her head, closer to the right side than the left, spilled over her shoulder as she moved. She appeared around thirty, with thin, soft features.

"I got hit a few times. Might have some bruises tomorrow," the one with the axe answered as if being shot was a minor irritation.

I moved back as they took away my cover. Soon the crates on one side of the room were all packed away. I had scurried behind the ones closer to the door. They hadn't touched them yet.

After the first truck was full the smaller woman and man left with a simple parting message from the woman, "Keep loading up the other truck. We'll take these and come back once we've got them unloaded."

With that they drove off.

Alone, the woman continued loading the second truck. Fortunately, there were too many boxes to fit them all in, leaving me with a small amount of cover. When she had filled it she sat down. I needed to find a way out or another place to hide before the others got back.

Then her phone rang. She pulled off the helmet, doing little more than brushing back the hair underneath. It was a mess of tangles, barely past shoulder length and falling partially in front of her face.

The phone was an old type that couldn't project a hologram and she held it up to her ear. *I suppose criminals would prefer privacy over face-to-face time.*

"What is it?" she spat out the words. Then her tone lowered, questioning, "Are you sure?"

Her eyes scanned the room. "Yeah, I've got it."

She put the phone away and my curiosity turned to dread as she reached back to grab the handle of her axe and stood up. *What is she doing?* I felt certain no one had seen me, and in a warehouse with one tiny window I wasn't concerned about being spotted from outside, either.

She hit a button to lower the garage door. Then she turned around.

As she began prowling around the room, axe hanging by her side, she searched around the truck, even getting down on one knee to check under it. She was definitely searching.

I glanced at the door, weighing my chances of outrunning her. The weight of her gear didn't seem to impede her, but it was still bulky and probably restricting. I hesitated, though. If I risked it and couldn't make it, there would be lethal consequences.

Each plodding step echoed in my head as she made her way towards the boxes and I inched the other way, trying to stay on the opposite side. I couldn't keep her in my sight but I heard her. I sneaked around the corner just as she moved behind them, standing with my back against a crate. I listened intently, resisting the temptation to peek out.

A thump on the side I used to be on urged me to make my way farther around. My fingers traced over the wooden crates as I slid by.

The steps paused on the other side, and so did I.

A box jammed into my back and shoved me forward. I stumbled away, trying to regain my balance and escape the tumbling crates. When I caught myself and looked back she was on the other side, looking over what was left of the pile.

In a pure panic I darted for the door, but she cut me off and I turned to run the other way. I didn't realize she had her gun out until I heard the shots. They rang out as I dove behind the truck. Using it for cover I patted myself to see if I'd been hit. *Nothing. Pressea's blessing.*

Her stomps approached and I ran towards the front. More shots blasted through the air when she rounded the back end just as I got to the front.

The click of her gun hit my ears. *Empty?* I checked, only to see her hands on the handle of her axe. I tried to swallow, to return my stomach to its proper place.

I was near the corner opposite the door. To get outside I'd have to run past her and hope I could keep a safe distance. If I kept this up, she would back me into a corner, though. I needed to get away somehow.

My eyes flicked over to the partially knocked-over boxes. Some were lying on the floor now but others were still stacked nearly to the ceiling. The rafters above caught my attention. *If she's out of bullets I could be safer up here.*

I made a mad dash for the crates and bounded up the stack. By the time I looked down she was right behind me. I reached up to grip one of the beams as she placed a foot on one of the boxes to stand on it.

It cracked. With her size, the armor and the axe on top of it, the crate couldn't support her weight and the wood splintered under her foot. She couldn't climb after me.

My relief was short-lived as she bashed boxes

out from under me. They teetered until the only thing holding me up was my grip on the beam.

I strained to haul myself up, barely throwing my feet up just as the axe flew up and struck the beam. The beam bounced from the force of it and I wobbled until it steadied. The axe clattered to the ground several yards away.

In the brief moment of safety, I looked for an escape. I climbed to the corner behind the truck to get out of sight as she followed. She walked with slow, lumbering steps, her eyes glaring up at me. If we waited too long her friends would come back and I'd have no chance.

Quiet overtook the room as she paced below and I shifted above. My heart pounded. I cowered in the corner of the ceiling, not seeing any way out. If I tried to get through the window she could grab me. No matter where I went I didn't see any way to climb somewhere fast enough to get away. I considered dropping down to the roof of the truck.

Then I heard my death sentence. The creak of someone climbing over the door on the other side of the room. Her friends were back. She looked over her shoulder and walking towards the back of the truck, slow and quiet.

"Leander?"

It was Valli's soft voice.

He came into view and I realized she was going to cut off his exit.

"Valli, run!" I warned him, but he seemed more startled than anything.

I watched in horror as he swiveled around and saw her. What could I do? Both of us combined probably couldn't outwrestle her.

He ran away with her on his tail, hefting up the axe with both hands. Valli was backed up against the wall with nowhere to run. Only his agility kept him alive as he dodged with extraordinary grace.

I have to do something. I hung down from the beam and dropped to the floor. I couldn't leave him there but what *could* I do?

My sights set on the truck next to me. I hopped in. Not knowing how to drive was the least of my worries right then. I climbed over the passenger's seat to the driver's and sat down. If only I'd paid attention to how Deckard worked it.

Turning the key brought it to life. The seat vibrated as the engine started. I turned from the dashboard to the window. Valli was desperately flailing to keep distance between him and the axe. He failed. It thrust into his chest, knocking him to the ground. Her attention switched to the truck.

I slammed my foot down on the pedal and clung to the wheel as it lurched forward. I tried to point it towards her but I had barely any space, time, or control. She moved back but the front corner hit her before I crashed into the wall.

I jumped out to grab Valli. He lay on his side, hand over his chest, as he struggled to push himself up. We had no time to check his injuries. I wrapped my arm around him and hefted him up as he groaned.

Despite his pain he stumbled along with me. It

was too much for him, though, and only I was keeping him from falling.

Without a thought, I swept him up into my arms and ran as fast as I could. Normally I doubted I could carry him far, if at all, but I had no choice.

"Are you okay?" I huffed out the words as I raced to the door.

"It feels like my muscles have been ripped from my chest," he groaned, face twisted in pain.

I checked to see where the giant was. She was still by the truck, but up on one knee, still moving. I couldn't get away while carrying him and he couldn't run. I needed to hide him somewhere and lead her away.

I carried him to the closest cover I could think of: the water heater outside the building.

"I was worried about you. I saw you go in, and then that person showed up, and chased a bunch of people out, and you didn't come back ..." His fingers dug into the clothing on his chest. "I called the police. They should be coming soon."

At least someone will be. I set him down behind the heater.

"I'm sorry, I can't run."

"It's okay," I tried to soothe him. "Just stay here and hide until the police get here. I'll lead her away. How badly are you hurt?"

I pulled open the top of his shirt, expecting to check his injuries, but underneath bandages were already wound tightly around his chest. He kept pressing his hand against it.

"I need to get to the hospital."

"You will. Just stay calm. Wait here. Help is coming." Guilt washed over me as I comforted him. I didn't want to leave him there, vulnerable, but if I stayed she would come for both of us. I had to keep her away from him. "I'm going to draw her away. Just stay quiet right here, okay?"

Between heavy, strained breaths, he nodded.

Guilt and fear made me linger, but I fought them off. He couldn't run and I couldn't defend him; my only choice was to lure her away. My fear wasn't for myself at this point. I was scared she wouldn't come after me. I was afraid her friends would come back and find him. I was terrified any number of things could happen to him the moment I left.

I jogged back to the front of the warehouse, looking for her. She was already stumbling through the doorway when I got there. *Now the tricky part. Making sure she follows me and not dying.*

Her eyes shot my way and I ran straight, away from Valli. If I could lose her in the brush and trees, I could double back around and get him.

I flew through the thickets, not caring about the prickles that grabbed at my pants. The dry air stung my lungs with every breath. I looked over my shoulder to see her giving chase. *Good. Now I just have to worry about staying alive.*

While I rushed through brush and trees, I kept peeking back. I felt some relief when I saw her limp as she followed me. Relentless as she was, I was faster. Each thistle that grabbed me gave me a fright, though. I

pushed farther, covering my face when I forced my way through overgrowth. At some point during the chase, I had no idea how long, I looked back and she was gone.

I slowed to a stop, listening, waiting, expecting her to catch up, but she didn't come. I felt dizzy after the run. No time for that, though.

As fast as my aching legs could carry me, I hurried back to the warehouse. I slowed as I approached it, partly because I was tired and partly because I needed to check the area. The garage door was open again, and when I peered inside, the second truck was missing. I didn't see anyone, though. I jogged around the backside as an extra precaution – I didn't want to run into any of the thug's friends by accident – and made my way to the water heater.

No one was there.

I looked all around but I didn't see Valli anywhere. No sign of the police, either. At the front of the warehouse I peeked inside. Still no one.

Don't panic. Maybe the police picked him up. I'll just go to the police station. They'd have to take him to the hospital, but I didn't know which one. I wasn't even sure how many hospitals were in the area.

My chest felt as if it were too small for my lungs the entire way back to town. *Please don't be dead, Valli.*

5

Anxiety ate at me during the journey to the police station. The idea that Valli might have been found by the gang stayed firmly chained to my mind, no matter how much I tried to brush it away and convince myself that the police had come. By the time I arrived at the station, the sky was a medium purple.

Inside, the back area was a maze of desks with a small reception area in the front. I greeted the officer in pink at the counter.

"Excuse me."

"Hello. How may I help you?" He folded his hands on the desk with a friendly smile.

"I wanted to ask about a call made earlier. My friend called about a warehouse about an hour ago. He was injured, and I wanted to check where he was."

The officer turned to his computer, browsing for a minute before turning back to me. "There's no such call here."

My breath hitched. Valli had no reason to lie about that. His own life was in danger, too, so it only made sense he would call. Why wouldn't there be a record?

"Are you sure?" I leaned over the desk.

He nodded. "I'm sure."

Then Valli …

"But he was really injured. If you guys didn't

find him then he must have been found by the black market people." As I rambled he stared at me, looking bored. "Please, you have to help him!"

"Please calm down. Tell me what information you can."

I went through the details, everything I knew, and he took some notes. After I finished, he looked up at me again and said, "The police will handle this. Please go back home and don't worry about it," without a hint of urgency.

I lingered at the desk. I wanted to do more, to say more, but what else could I do or say? I'd given the information. I had to go.

I meandered through the town, mind racing, struggling with how to proceed next. The only clue I'd gotten from Ellora was the location of one warehouse. I'd seen people there but didn't know who they were. And then Valli was gone, and the truck was gone, and I didn't know where any of them went.

Instinct told me to head back towards the warehouse but I couldn't think of anything I would find there. I ended up on a cart riding towards the edge of the city anyway. With my cheek resting in the palm of my hand I stared out the window, barely registering anything outside until bright white stood out in the dim evening. *Soldier uniforms?*

The thought was comforting. Dad, Rykiel, and so many other people I grew up around, were soldiers. When I mulled it over, the idea became more foreboding. Soldiers rarely came this far north. *General Glaive?* I stood up to get a better view of the spot the cart had gone by, running to the back window. It was a large building with decorative pillars. A town hall or something.

I recalled Glaive's men back at the restaurant. Why were they here? Did they know about the gangs?

Then it hit me. The item Ellora had told me to go after was the king's coronation necklace. If we had heard about it maybe they had too. It belonged to the castle; did they come to get it back? Sending the general to retrieve it seemed overzealous but, perhaps out of desperation, my mind forced a connection. If there was, I had a chance of finding more information here.

I stuck my ID card in the slot by the door and rushed through the menu to pick a new destination just down the street. I held onto a bar as it slowed to a stop and flew out the second the door opened. My mind told me I was being foolish but my heart clung to hope.

I darted to the town hall, watching the small group enter the building. I saw the tail end. Quinn, Giddeon, Tyrus ... No doubt they were all there. I needed to find a way to listen in.

All the lights were off. If I hadn't seen them enter, I would have assumed the building was closed. I inched towards the front door and peeked in one of the windows. The whole front of the building was dark.

The door was unlocked when I turned the knob. I stepped inside, closing it behind me. I hadn't realized how chilly it was outside until warm air suddenly overtook me. My mind had been too preoccupied.

I didn't know my way around the building so I trailed my fingers along the wall as I walked. At least five elite soldiers were in here somewhere. I needed to be careful.

When I rounded a corner, I spotted two of them facing away from me, down the hall. I ducked into the room next to me.

Tyrus' ear flicked. I could tell it was him because only he had hair like mine.

Like before, Dorrius was the one by him. He caught the flick immediately. "What is it?"

"I thought I heard something. Probably just the wind." He glanced behind. I moved completely into the room.

"No," Dorrius corrected him. "The General is very detail oriented. He likes to make certain of everything. Where did you hear it?"

"I'm not sure. Just in one of those rooms somewhere," Tyrus replied.

"Then let's check them," Dorrius said.

I didn't have much time. I found a cabinet and opened it, rolling inside and barely closing the doors before Tyrus came in. He paused when he stepped inside, eyes scouring the room. Dorrius went into the room across from my hiding spot. I heard doors being opened and shut.

Tyrus was more hesitant as he moved around the table, glancing under it, his hand on top of it when he knelt down. When he stood back up, he shuffled around the room, seemingly confused. Due to my small stature I could squeeze into spots most people couldn't and I hoped it would keep him from finding me.

A minute later Dorrius came into the room as

well.

"Did you find anything?"

Tyrus shook his head. "No."

"All right." Dorrius accepted the answer. "Then let's head back."

"Aren't you going to double check it?" Tyrus sounded perplexed.

"We have to be able to rely on you," he said, repeating the question more firmly, "Is the room clear?"

Tyrus' eyes wandered around the room before he answered, "Yes."

Dorrius nodded, turning to head back into the hall. "You'll understand better once you finish the light bulb test."

"… That one is driving me crazy."

Their voices faded down the hallway. I spilled out of the cabinet onto the floor. *That was close.*

I stuck my head into the hallway and looked both ways. Clear.

Each step felt like it could be my last. I tested each spot on the floor to make sure it wouldn't squeak before I moved forward. I wondered if it was a fruitless effort, though. The only way to test if it would make a sound would be to make a sound.

Down another hall, the only light I'd seen on the entire time shone through the cracks of a large double door. No sign of anyone. I heard muffled voices and hoped they covered any sound I made. As I got closer I could make out their conversation.

"You were still a boy the last time we were able

to talk like this. Do you remember the book I gave you?"

I peered through the crack between the doors. General Glaive's back was to me. Seven feet tall with a muscular body and combed-back hair, he would be hard to mistake for anyone else even from behind. He stood in front of a desk where the noble Darora Seer sat. Darora had been the one speaking in a conversational tone, remarkably relaxed considering who he was facing. I couldn't see whether anyone else was in the room.

"Are you under the impression I came here to make friends? I don't appreciate having to come here to clean up your mess," Glaive's response was cold and I winced in sympathy for Darora.

The General's blunt reply caused his previously calm expression to stiffen, but he managed to keep himself composed. "It's a difficult situation, General. General Oske understands."

"Do I look like General Oske?"

Darora paused before speaking cautiously, "With all due respect, General Glaive, I think I'd prefer to discuss this with General Oske. Where is he?"

The general didn't hesitate. "At the castle, where he always is."

"He has decades of experience. I'm sure he would be better equipped to deal with this." Darora strained to keep a level tone.

"He's the one who allowed it to go this far in the first place."

He stood, arms folded, head high, and spoke

without reserve even when it was about General Oske.

"I don't think you understand the gravity of the situation. We're talking about thousands of people. This would be difficult for anyone to handle."

"Your territory only has three hundred thousand people total. I'm responsible for three hundred million."

"Don't you mean the king is?"

There was a half-second pause before Glaive responded, "Of course."

"I know you're the new General, but I've been overseeing this territory since you were a toddler. You have to show a little respect."

"This area has been slowly falling apart since I was a toddler. I don't intend to let that continue. If I have to replace you to do that, then I will."

"General Glaive!" He stood from his desk but his stature didn't compare to the General's. "You don't need to make such presumptuous statements. I've served for several decades. Twee can attest to my standing."

"Don't attempt to hide behind Twee. He's a respectable man but his children are idiots. He's too focused on trying to assure they won't be stripped of their positions to worry about you." He tilted his head, gesturing towards Darora. "A position I'm sure you can empathize with."

His scalding remark quieted Darora. His reply had a more subdued anger than his previous outrage, "It's not polite to call his children idiots."

"Do you disagree with my assessment?" Glaive

challenged him.

Darora answered with silence.

"Then don't waste time arguing semantics with me," he held up a hand while he scolded Darora.

"This is no way to discuss politics." Darora fell back in his chair with a sigh.

"I'm not a politician. I'm a soldier. You can move to Rhodaren if you want to waste time with endless discussions that lead nowhere. I'm sure many of the other nobles would be glad to have this territory if you can't handle it," Glaive warned him.

"I can handle it. We've run it for generations, we don't need any help." Anxiety leaked through the noble's voice.

"Murders, kidnappings and violent attacks have been increasing every year."

"We've just been having some difficult years with some ... degenerates," his voice trembled. "We'll get it under control."

"You've had plenty of time to try, Darora. The security of the country is my job."

The noble brought a hand to his head. No doubt he was feeling the pressure talking to the general. The fact that Glaive could have whomever he wanted killed would be intimidating even if he was a gentle man. The king was technically the highest position, but most people considered the king and general almost equal. They even shared the same floor of the castle.

"I understand," the words sounded disingenuous. "The local police force is at your disposal. You should have enough manpower to handle the situation with them."

"I've already informed them of our plans. We'll be heading to a warehouse close to Vale to round up part of the gang infestation tomorrow at noon."

The noble bolted upright, flustered. "You spoke to the police before me?"

"It seemed pertinent. Once we clean out the infestation you'll have to make preparations to prevent it from happening again." Glaive sounded more like he was giving orders than explaining. "If you can't do it, I'll gladly put Searess in charge. I'm sure she could."

"You can't do that! She hardly has any experience!"

"Even kings can be replaced," Glaive bit back. It was an old saying but a well-known one. "Searess's territory has been doing exceptionally well and her younger son seems competent. I'm sure she'd be happy to have a place secured for his future."

"I assure you, that won't be necessary." Darora was nothing more than a wide-eyed lympet backed into a corner.

"We'll see. I'll meet with you again once I've finished the job."

The noble seemed relieved when he leaned back in the chair. No small talk followed. As soon as the general began turning around, I knew I needed a hiding spot. Fast. I worried about the noise I made when I ran, but I had little time.

I turned into the first room I came across and dove behind a counter, praying for the best.

Moments later their footsteps marched through

the hallway. They kept going, and once they faded, I breathed a sigh of relief and stood up. Surely I could sneak out the other way, through a window if I had to.

I whirled around the door to go the other way but ran face first into something cushy and white. Stunned, I stepped back. It felt like minutes before I looked up to see Dorrius was standing right next to the doorway. I twirled to bolt for it but Quinn was on the other side.

I was caught. Dorrius grabbed my arm and dragged me back to the room I'd been spying on just minutes before. By the now-abandoned desk, I spun around to face them as soon as he released my arm and ended up in front of the general himself. I only came up to his shoulder. His troops stood at either of my sides, taller than me – even Tyrus, by a little bit. They didn't concern themselves with me as Dorrius focused more on Tyrus. I heard him whispering to the other man, mouth to his ear, "You see how we have to work as a team. The general wants us to know each other inside and out, so that we can read each other without ever saying a word."

Tyrus stayed silent as he gazed at the other man with a quizzical expression.

"Your ID." General Glaive held out a hand expectantly. No point in trying to hide it. I dug my ID out of my jacket and handed it over. I felt like a little forgbug looking up at him, waiting for him to tear me apart and roast me.

He gestured to the chair behind the desk. My eyes followed before looking back to him for reassurance.

"Have a seat. You'll be here for a while," he said. I faced him while I sidled over to the chair, my hands hovering above the desk before finally giving in and touching it as I sat down. I didn't want to be in Darora's spot.

"Your name," he demanded, composed even as a hint of irritation shaded his voice.

"Leander."

"What are you doing here?" He folded his arms. Now I knew how Darora felt, feeling minuscule in front of this colossal man.

Nothing could keep me calm. I didn't want to disappear never to be seen again. My voice – no, my whole body -- shook when I answered, "I saw you come inside and I was curious what was happening ..."

"What are you doing in the area?"

Even if anxiety wasn't overwhelming me I doubted I could get away lying to the general, so I told as much of the truth as I could, "I came here with a friend to help him while he got surgery. It's been boring waiting in the hotel, though ..."

"His name?"

He was asking the questions so quickly I had no time to think before answering. "Valli."

"Where are you from?"

"The capital."

"And the friend?"

"He's from the capital, too. He works at the Lambrian Theater." I hoped the mention of the Wind

Queen's theater would reflect positively on me.

He held my ID to the side and Tetchion took it from his hand. "Check his story."

Tetchion glanced down at my ID and left without a word, leaving me there with the other five. My eyes darted around the group. Despite the publicly released information, I didn't know anything about their personalities; I had no idea what to expect.

I just needed to get out of there so I could try to find Valli. While his troops went about their business on the other side of the room – Quinn whispering to Giddeon, Giddeon shoving Quinn's shoulder, Dorrius glancing at them impassively and Tyrus cowering on the other side of Dorrius, away from the others – Glaive stayed in front of the desk. Having his eyes bearing down on me made me want to crawl under the desk so he couldn't see me, but I had a feeling he might be the type to walk around and keep staring just to make me uncomfortable. I searched for things to look at on the wall, doing anything to avoid meeting his stare.

General Glaive was a man wrapped in a million rumors. "He's a genius." "He has a photographic memory." "He's undefeated in combat." "He scored a perfect 15 on the GICH test."

Then there were the other rumors. "He's sadistic." "He collects torture devices." "The men who don't pass his interview, disappear." "He scored a perfect 15 because the examiners were too scared to give him anything lower." "He never smiles."

I knew, at least, that last one wasn't true. I had met him once, albeit briefly. Yet somehow, without a single word ever passing between us, I had made him smile.

6

Even as an eight-year-old child it was difficult to deter me once I had my mind set on something. One day, about ten years before, I made a decision; it was just a matter of convincing my dad.

During his break from work I swooped in to negotiate with paper in hand. He was relaxing on the couch, one arm on the armrest and the other holding a book.

"Dad!" I called him but got no response. It did nothing to dissuade me. "Dad!" I grabbed his knee and shook it. "Dad! Dad!"

Still nothing. I climbed up on the couch next to him and pushed on his arm with my feet, putting all my weight into it. "Daaaaaaaaaad!"

It was clear by then that he was pointedly ignoring me but I wouldn't be ignored. I rolled onto my stomach and turned around to head butt his arm, digging my feet into the couch and lunging forward as I repeated in a lower, guttural tone, "Dad!"

He finally looked my way as if he just noticed me. "Oh, did you want something?"

That was the only opening I needed. I shoved the paper in his face.

"This!"

He eyed the advertisement for a model of the castle, never taking it. A grunt escaped him before he answered, "I can't afford that."

I wasn't falling for that. He brushed off all attempts to negotiate that day so I printed out copies of the advertisement and hung them all over the house that night. Unfortunately, he was unrelenting and took them down the next morning without a word.

Finally he took me with him to the office, where I could find reinforcements. Rykiel was working at the counter, as usual.

I always liked Rykiel. I liked most of Dad's fellow soldiers, but Rykiel especially. As far back as I could remember I had always wanted him to like me. I couldn't place any particular reason why -- maybe it was just because he worked as a receptionist for the base, so I saw him the most.

While they were discussing Dad's schedule and upcoming re-training Rykiel turned towards me with a smile.

"You seem upset today, Leander. What's wrong?"

I slapped a copy of the advertisement on top of the counter which I could barely see over.

"Dad won't buy me this."

"Uh-oh, Lorough, Leander is telling on you." Rykiel looked it over with a curious hum, then gently tried to explain, "Ah, I see. But fancy models like this usually cost a lot of money. Your dad might not be able to afford that."

"No," I corrected him, pointing at a spot on the ad. "He bought a real house, and this is only 1/100 the size so it should only be 1/100 the price."

He laughed. "Is *that* how it works?" He looked at my dad and continued in good humor, "You're holding out on him."

I glanced up at my dad who rolled his eyes with a sigh, muttering under his breath, "I'm still paying for that house."

"One one hundredth of the size of the castle ... That would still be pretty big, wouldn't it? Around three feet or so?" Rykiel mused, eyes on my dad as he held a hand at the height of his hip.

"About that size," Dad agreed.

"You know, Leander," Rykiel leaned on the counter to lower himself closer to my height, "that's a nice model, but wouldn't you like to see the *real* castle?"

My eyes widened. There was only one answer for that. "Yeah!"

Continuing to be unreasonable, my dad butted in, speaking in an uncertain tone, "Aren't the tours there pretty expensive?"

Continuing to be awesome, though, Rykiel already had it all figured out. "Not if you're a soldier. You work for the government, and the castle is just the main base of operations. Technically you work for the castle. Let me get a pamphlet."

Finally my dad softened to the idea when Rykiel handed him a pamphlet he'd dug out.

"You could even rent a room in the castle if you wanted." He chuckled as my dad grimaced and shook his head at that idea.

I took in a breath, stunned. "We should move into the castle!"

Dad wrinkled his nose and reached down to take my hand and head home. "We'd only have one room if we moved into the castle."

"But we'd be living in *the castle!*"

"We're not living in the castle," he answered flatly, glaring at Rykiel and yelling back, "I'm going to buy your daughter a recorder when she gets older."

Rykiel just chuckled softly. I didn't understand it was a threat at the time.

Days later we went to the castle for the tour. I'd seen the front many times before. Rows of giant white pillars with flowers planted at the base. Between the planters, water flowed like an endless fountain. Statues of the former generals stood in line, visible through the gaps in the pillars as they kept a vigilant guard over the castle.

The tour started by the rows of statues, down halls full of golden engravings. Even Dad started to get into it. Near the entrance to the castle, he knelt down beside me, pointing out the general nearest to the entrance on the right.

"That's Luenlore. She's the one who replaced the previous line of royalty when they became corrupt." He pointed up at the statue. "It was a few generations before people discovered what really happened, because back then most people would never see the king. She picked the person who replaced the king and she was probably the one really running the country." I looked up at the giant statue expecting to see the Luenlore from fairy tales. Instead her face was as cold and hard as the marble it was made of.

We toured the base of the castle, seeing some of the hundreds of rooms. Dad held my hand while we were guided through, but I wanted to go higher up and see more of the castle.

Then it caught my eye. Down a hallway, a servant pushed a cart off an elevator. If I could get on the elevator, I could go to the top of the castle and look down at the entire city.

While the group moved on, I slowed. Dad didn't notice at first, letting my hand slip from his as I stopped. They peered into the next room, each trying to get a peek as the tour guide ushered them into the large hallway and explained what it was used for. That's when I made a break for it and caught his attention.

"Leander!" Dad called out and instantly chased after me.

The elevator wasn't far; I just needed a good enough head start. I ran as fast as my legs would go, but he grabbed my arm right in front of it. "Leander! What do you think you're doing?"

Just as he began scolding me the elevator reached the bottom yet again, but this time it wasn't a servant. General Oske himself stepped out, closely followed by a teen-aged Glaive. The General still had both eyes at the time and was an impressive seven feet, four inches tall.

Dad's eyes widened as he dropped down to one knee and tugged me out of the way, bowing his head. "I'm sorry, Sir. I have him." Both of his arms wrapped around me.

General Oske glared down at him, his

expression hard and his voice tinged with annoyance. "Lack of discipline is a sign of poor parenting."

My dad gave no response, gritting his teeth and keeping his head low as the General walked by. Glaive quietly followed, marching like any other soldier behind him.

He insulted my dad. I didn't care who he was, he couldn't do that! I overcame my shock and scowled at him, pulling away from my dad as I shouted after him, "You're wrong! My dad is the best dad in the world!"

A hand slapped over my mouth when Dad grabbed me. The General paused and glanced over his shoulder. Dad stared up at him, ears down, taking some rapid breaths. Without a word the General continued down the hall. I felt my dad's forehead press against my back as he sighed, eyes on the floor.

I kept glaring down the hallway as they walked away. Glaive turned his head and I gave my best defiant look, expecting him to be scowling. Instead he had a smirk on his face. A strange, bemused smirk. I stared after him in confusion, and although he never said a single word his unsettling smile stayed with me.

7

An eternity passed before Glaive's man returned. I watched the others interact while we waited. Glaive himself stayed in place silently, but his men had picked out a table to play some sort of training game on. From my spot I could see that they'd set up a holographic map and were moving virtual troops around it.

They explained to Tyrus which unit he could control as they started. Gideon and Quinn played on the Geuranian side while Dorrius and Tyrus played on the Naggian side.

Immediately after Tyrus began making moves, he was corrected.

"You can't do that. Your troops would be picked off while climbing up the mountain path." Dorrius pointed at the path Tyrus was leading them towards.

"But they could flank the Geuranians from over here." Tyrus pointed further.

"You can't sacrifice troops to do that. The point is to win without losing any soldiers."

"Isn't that impossible?"

"It's our job," Dorrius stated.

"If you don't want to deal with as many rules you can play on the Geuranian side," Quinn snickered, rolling his head to look at Giddeon. "We can't count on them to care what happens to their troops."

Giddeon and Tyrus traded places after that, putting Dorrius and Giddeon on the Naggian side and Tyrus and Quinn on the Gueranian side. They continued on until Tyrus apparently made another controversial move.

"You can't do that!" Giddeon spoke up with a mixture of surprise and confusion.

"Well, he's on the Gueranian side, so technically it isn't against the rules," Quinn defended him, but he sounded unsure himself.

"He'll lose too many troops that way, though," Giddeon complained.

Dorrius held up a hand, quieting them. "No, it's fine. It isn't against the rules."

"But it's too reckless," Giddeon protested.

"When the Geuranians attacked our capital they knew they would lose hundreds, if not thousands, of troops. We can't depend on them not being willing to sacrifice their troops," Dorrius explained to Giddeon calmly. "This is good. We've grown used to playing defensively. It's our own fault that we overlooked the pass because we assumed no one would go there."

Giddeon's expression slackened, passing a few doubtful glances between the other two. Dorrius stayed sitting tall, while Quinn studied the map, rubbing his chin. Tyrus, who remained silent the whole time, slumped in his seat like he was trying to make himself smaller.

The game went much differently after that. They spent a lot of time mulling over their options. It managed to distract me from my own situation. At least I knew they wouldn't gamble with my dad's life. It was unusual to hear, though. Winning without losing a single life ... I had to agree with Tyrus, it sounded impossible.

Footsteps echoing down the hallway yanked me back to reality. Tetchion pushed through the door and walked straight to Glaive, handing my ID to him.

"His story checks out. He arrived a few days ago with a man from the theater who is scheduled to have surgery and has shown up to appointments. Members of the staff recall seeing him with a friend," Tetchion informed Glaive, but his pitch went up a miniscule amount when he added, "No criminal record."

Tyrus, tired of poring over strategies, approached from his seat with a renewed spark of interest. "So what are we going to do to him?"

To me? My fingers clenched the seat.

"Nothing," the General answered, accepting the ID. Tyrus's expression sank. When General Glaive continued, he sounded critical of Tyrus's reaction, "He's a mischievous boy. It's not worth our time."

The General placed my ID flat on the table in front of me, his fingers lingering on top of it. I didn't dare reach to take it back. He glared down at me as he gave me some advice, "Your enthusiasm for politics is appreciated but will get you hurt. Go home and be a good, productive citizen."

His hand slid away from my ID and he stood up straight, hands behind his back. Fearful he'd smack my hand if I reached for it, I watched him with wary eyes when I picked it up. I heard one last thing as I scurried out.

"It's going to be a long night."

My thought exactly. Night had fallen while I was inside. I wanted so badly to go back out and search for Valli, but I could hardly see and was too tired to be of any use. General Glaive and the rest of this group were going to be at the warehouse tomorrow, so I would avoid that ruckus.

That left the spot the woman wielding the axe had mentioned. If I could find that place, maybe I'd make some progress.

I got back to the hotel in a slump, physically and emotionally spent. How could I sleep when Valli was out there, hurt? He could be sitting in the cold right now, or worse, dead. *No, I can't think that.* I had to believe he was alive.

It felt wrong to be at the hotel while he was still out there, in danger. It took several minutes of convincing myself before I took a bath. Staying dirty wasn't going to help him. Neither would being sleep deprived.

Even if the police told me to stay home and let them handle it, I couldn't do that. Tomorrow I'd go back out and look for him for sure. I wouldn't stop until I found him.

That night I had a dream.

I sat in my living room in the dead of night. I kept my eyes on the windows, unsettled by the darkness.

Then something scraped along the ground outside. A shudder ran through my body. A scraper? I didn't want to see the monster face to face. They were known for scheming and setting traps.

I leaned close to the window to see as much as I could and the empty world just intensified my dread. Even though I didn't see anything outside I knew something was lurking out there. Heart pounding, I ran down to my dad's room and locked the door at the top of the stairs. He was on his bed, reading.

"Dad, something's out there." I climbed onto the bed next to him.

He didn't listen at all, no matter how many times I warned him. The most I got was a few hummed responses, pretending that he was listening to me while he read. I wanted to run away but I couldn't. I couldn't leave Dad there. I wanted him to get up. I wanted him to protect me.

As he ignored my pleas, something started pounding on the door at the top of the stairs. My fingers dug into his arm. I crouched down lower on the bed. I couldn't understand why my dad still showed no concern.

While I sat on the bed, eyes glued to the stairs and listening to each echoing thump with bated breath, I awoke, startled.

The lingering fear slowly faded away as I became conscious.

The first thing that occurred to me was Dad's absence. I caught sight of the other bed. Valli was gone, too. I'd never felt so alone.

I didn't feel any better than when I went to bed. My nerves were frazzled. I couldn't shake the reality that Valli might be dead. I didn't even get to check his wounds under the bandages ...*Why was he wearing bandages anyway? He hadn't gotten surgery yet.*

No, that didn't matter. I needed *something* to calm me. The v-phone looked so inviting. I couldn't tell Dad exactly what happened, but I could at least talk to him before I left.

I plunked down and called him. My mind was too preoccupied to even come up with a good excuse. I just needed someone.

"Good morning," he answered cheerfully right away.

"Mornin'," I sniffed.

He caught on right away, his expression becoming puzzled. "What's wrong?"

"Things didn't … go well last night." I aimed for vague, covering half my face with my hand. There was no hiding how upset I was.

"Your friend's surgery didn't go well?"

I shook my head.

"That's too bad," he answered sympathetically, brows furrowed. "But they have great hospitals there. Whatever is wrong, he's in the best hands he could possibly be. I'm sure he'll be fine."

"You really think so?"

It didn't matter that he knew nothing about the situation. I needed to hear it.

"I'm sure. He'll be okay. Just do whatever you can to help him," he encouraged me.

I gave a small nod. I couldn't stay there long, though. I had important work to get to. "I have to go."

My dad nodded. "Take care. I love you."

"I love you, too," I said quickly before turning

off the v-phone.

I gathered my things and stopped to look up directions. It took some investigating, but I discovered the Mosley was another warehouse located outside the city. Another one of their dens ... I imagined it would be filled with more of their stashed goods.

I inhaled deeply. No matter what was there, I had to go. If Valli was alive, I had to bring him back.

More people could be there and I might be able to get some information. It was my only lead.

I rode a cart to the edge of the city, then continued on foot. It took over thirty minutes to walk there, but my natural sense of direction kept me on target. It was, indeed, another warehouse, similar to the first with a few noticeable differences. A storage shed sat to the side of this one. It also looked bigger. Maybe it had more rooms inside.

While I pondered how to enter without being caught, I spotted something else. The door was locked on the outside. I picked up the large, dangling lock and jiggled it as if there were any chance I could break it. No good. I wouldn't be getting in through the door. There were still windows, though. I turned to the storage shed. This time I might be able to get a ladder.

I jogged over to it. It was beaten down and unsecured. The door scraped the ground when it opened. I found a small ladder inside, along with piles of old, worn tools and outdoor equipment. Good enough for what I needed. I brushed aside webs and grabbed the ladder, dragging it with me to the window on the side of the warehouse. I dug the bottom of it into the soil to hold it in place.

Once it seemed steady enough, I climbed my way up. I forced the shoddy latch open and shoved the window in.

What I saw inside stunned me. Dozens of people filled the space, but they weren't like the people at the other warehouse. Most looked young, from early to late teens. They all sat in front of sewing machines, working on clothing and bags. They didn't seem threatening, at least. A pair stopped working to look up at me, while others glanced up and instantly got back to work.

"Who are you?" one young woman asked.

"Um ... Leander. I was just looking for a friend." I scanned the room. I didn't see Valli. "Did anyone bring a boy here the other day?"

"Yeah, two. One's whiny. They're in the back." the woman gestured towards the back wall, oddly calm about their situation.

"Are you guys stuck here?" It felt like a stupid question to ask, but the lack of panic boggled my mind. Of course I remembered the lock on the front door. They couldn't get out.

"That's the way of things," an older woman called out over her before she got a chance to answer. I guessed her age at about thirty, but their sickly appearances made it difficult to be sure.

"Do you need help?" I felt obligated to ask even if I didn't have a plan of action.

"No one's gonna help us," the same woman answered. Her eyes never turned away from her work.

I furrowed my brows. "I could tell the police."

She huffed, "Don't be stupid. The police aren't going to help. They're just as corrupt as the rest of them."

"What?" I stared in shock, but as I mulled it over … Valli had called the police and they denied he made a call. Why would Valli lie about calling? No one knew I was inside of the warehouse either, until shortly before Valli came inside. If he made the call before that, then were they the ones who informed that axe woman I was there? They never came to rescue us, either.

I shook my head. Regardless of that, *I* knew they were here, and I'd make sure they got help one way or another.

"Don't worry, I'll get you out," I promised.

"This is how it is. Don't try to get people's hopes up," she scoffed. "You're going to get killed if you even try."

"You mean by that person with the axe?"

"Axe isn't the one you've gotta worry about." For the first time she looked up at me. Stress lines had permanently ingrained themselves on her face. "She's soft on us. Hard on gang members."

I didn't bother asking for clarification on who "Axe" was. It left me confused, though. In my brief encounter with her she didn't seem soft on anyone. "Why?"

"Probably because she used to be one of us," she stated flatly before turning back to her work. Her tone had a tense feel to it, as if her patience was long worn out.

"She was?" I was surprised again. They looked underfed and weak. She didn't fit that description at all.

A young man spoke up eagerly, "Yeah, but then one day she chopped up a bunch of them. She hasn't been working in here since."

The first girl next to him piped up again, "I'm going to be like Axe."

"Why would you want to be like *her*?" I asked, baffled.

The man stopped his sewing, looking up at me. "Because she got out."

"Knock it off and get your work done. I'm not getting in trouble because of you," the woman butted in again. "Soft or not, she has no patience for slackers."

I was perplexed. I couldn't imagine any way these people would overpower anyone.

"How did she get out?"

"I'll tell you how." The woman somehow managed to sound even more irate. "I was the only one of us around back then, so don't listen to any of these guys. It was eight years ago." Even as she spoke her hands worked mechanically, never stopping. "She found out her parents had another kid and decided to make a break for it. Wanted to get the kid and go somewhere better, but she got caught. They brought her in to show us what happens when someone tries to escape, toddler in her arms and all. We all hid in the back, and by the time we came out they were all chopped up and she and the kid were gone."

I was still confused. "But where'd she get the

axe?"

"It's a replica. They decided to try and counterfeit ancient weapons at the time. You know, like swords of old generals, selling them off as the real thing. Guess they didn't worry about it too much since they had guns, and guns win against swords and knives, right?" Her lip twitched up in the corner and she let out one amused laugh. "Maybe not every time."

"Then … why is she still here?" *The entire point had been to escape, right?*

"Ask her if you want to know," she snapped at me. "Can't you see we have work to do here?"

I shrank away from her. I didn't have time for this, either. After I checked on Valli, I would figure out some way to get them all to safety.

I slid down to the ground and carried the ladder to the back of the warehouse, where another window was. Two new boys were supposed to be back here. I climbed up to the window only to discover they really were *boys*. One looked around five or six and the other around ten. The younger had a partially-made bag sitting on his lap as he fiddled with it. He had tears in his eyes, cuts on his hands and a flushed face. The older one knelt by him and tried to help.

They were startled when I opened the window, both looking up. The older one had a trim figure with long hair, while the little one had a stocky shape with a short puff of hair.

"Are you the new people here?" I asked.

"Ah … yeah," the older one mumbled, lips pursed, while the smaller rubbed at his eyes.

"But you're so young!"

"I'm not young. I'm nine." He puffed out his chest.

"And I'm six." The smaller followed suit, stating it as if it were a large number even though his eyes were still swollen and red.

"What are you doing in a place like this?"

"We got grabbed in our home and they took us here," the older said.

I drew my brows together and tightened my grip on the windowsill. I'd only ever heard of things like this, like they only happened in other countries. I had no idea anyone could get away with this here. I tried to hold in my anger because I wasn't mad at them and I didn't want to yell at them.

"How can they bring you guys here? He can barely even do that!" I spat it out too harshly, indicating the mess of materials that were forming a bag-like shape.

"I'll help him. I learned to sew at the mansion," the older tried to reassure me.

The little one walked over to the wall, looking up at me. "Are you going to get us out?"

I need to get them somewhere safe. Ideas ran through my head. If the police were no good, then where else could I go? There was always Child Services, but I couldn't contact them from here and I wondered if they could deal with this situation. As much as I feared General Glaive, he was another possibility. If nothing else, I felt confident he didn't have any connection to this, especially since he seemed so adamant about capturing the gang.

General Glaive! The thought reminded me of what I heard the night before. He'd said they would be at the other warehouse at noon, and he'd spoken to the police. *And the police are corrupt.*

I needed to warn them; they might be ambushed.

"I have to do something, but I'll come back and help get you guys back home, okay? Just wait here."

"Are you really going to come back?" he cried in fear.

"I promise. Just keep safe for now," I assured him.

They seemed to have more hope in their eyes than the other captives did. "Okay."

I felt bad leaving them there but told myself it was temporary. I'd go warn the general and his troops, then get help for the boys. I slid to the ground and put the ladder back to hide any evidence that I'd been there.

With a few hours before noon, I ran as much as I could to the first warehouse, slowing to a walk when I needed to rest. The gang members would likely show up sooner than the soldiers in order to prepare a trap for them, so I needed to intercept them and warn them. If they came from the city, I knew the general direction they had to travel from.

By the time I arrived, my throat was parched. I wiped my forehead with the back of my hand and pushed forward. I didn't see any signs of someone being at the warehouse yet. The garage door was closed but the front door had been fixed, which surprised me. I didn't expect them to care about a broken door on an old building. It looked like sturdy metal one, too.

I pressed my ear to it but didn't hear a thing inside. *No one is here yet?* Opening the door, I poked my head in. The warehouse looked the same as before, but it was empty now save for a single crate sitting next to the back wall.

Curiosity prodded me until I walked into the building to check the crate. Strolling through an empty building where I had been attacked before had an eerie feeling to it. I placed a hand on the wooden lid and pulled it up. Garments filled it. Nothing special.

"Hey." A voice echoed through the room. I jumped and swiveled, afraid it would be a gang member. Instead Dorrius stood in the doorway.

"What are you doing here?" he asked. His voice had a gentle firmness to it, demanding but not angry.

"I ..." I was so stressed out tears built in the corners of my eyes. "I just came to warn you! The police are corrupt, so the gang probably knows you're coming but ... you're already here."

Several lights on a small device hanging from his hip blinked. He glanced at it.

He didn't seem to be listening to me, replying calmly as he approached, "You need to leave before it gets dangerous. Get out and head south, up the hill and into the brush."

I couldn't leave it at that. If the police really were corrupt he *needed* to listen to me. "Please! I'm telling the truth!"

He took my arm, tugging me a few steps towards the door. "Go. We need to do our job."

I didn't dare defy his orders. I looked to him with desperation in my eyes, but he met them with a stiff glare. I hoped he at least took my warning into account. Dorrius told me a specific location to go to. I didn't know why, but I didn't know where else to go, either, so I followed his directions. There was something soothing about following a clear order instead of bungling around.

I ran across the field, occasionally peeking back. Dorrius stood outside the warehouse, not straying far. *But I didn't see him when I got here. And I don't see any of the others.*

I climbed through the familiar brush. General Glaive was there, stationed behind some cover. He had the same blinking item sitting in front of him as he focused on the warehouse. At first I stayed back. His eyes flicked towards me for a split second, so he knew I was there, but he didn't say a word.

What should I do? Am I in trouble? My stomach did somersaults, pestering me to leave, but my legs refused to move.

If Dorrius wouldn't listen to me, maybe the general would. He didn't seem to be paying me much mind, but I cautiously approached him.

"G-General Glaive, sir." I inwardly yelled at myself for stammering. "I ... I heard that the police are corrupt, so if you told them your plans then the gang probably knows, too."

His eyes darted my way momentarily before he said one low sentence, "Sit and be quiet." He continued keeping watch.

"Please, I'm telling the truth," I pleaded, both desperate and quiet, "There's another warehouse with people locked inside and they told me the police were corrupt!"

"We know," he answered.

I gawked. "You do?"

"It's all corrupt here. From the police to the orphanages. It will be fixed this week." He looked away from his post briefly to meet my eyes. "Now sit and be quiet."

Confused, I fell back on my butt, waiting. *They knew? Then why did they talk to the police before?*

I noticed the blinking lights again. Five lights, like the other one. One would start blinking then stop, or sometimes two. He flipped small switches on them before pressing a little button at the top several times. A code?

I peered through the brush that he was staring through. I didn't see Dorrius anymore. The warehouse looked abandoned.

While my eyes were turned, General Glaive surprised me when he suddenly spoke, but it wasn't to me.

"Stop telling jokes, Quinn. Concentrate."

My attention immediately went back to him. After a moment, he flicked the last switch up and spoke again, "That made no sense, Tyrus. If you don't remember how to use it then just use one for yes, two for no. Are you ready?"

The last light blinked once.

Somehow I'd always pictured the general dealing with things by bursting in with guns blazing, taking everyone out. Watching him sit in the distance, observing in silence, was strange. I still didn't have a clue where his men even were.

Time dragged. It dragged until I grew old and withered away, or at least it felt like it. It was probably an hour later that something happened.

A truck appeared in the distance. I recognized it as the type the gang used. It pulled up to the building and stopped in front of it. Before I knew it, I was leaning forward, wanting to see what would happen next.

The passenger left the vehicle, going inside of the building. A bit later they came back out, said something to the driver, and both moved into the building. Not long after that, one walked back outside again, looking at the garage door and banging on it a few times.

People began pouring out of the back of the truck, seemingly wondering what was taking so long as they wandered over. They gestured angrily at the garage door. Finally, they decided on a solution. Everyone in the back of the truck was ushered out, carrying their equipment with them, and the driver drove the truck away while everyone else filed into the warehouse.

We watched the driver make a long walk from wherever he parked the truck back to the warehouse. I looked to General Glaive, wondering when he was going to do something. After a long trek the man joined the others in the building.

That was when the general suddenly made a move. He began sending signals rapidly.

Beside the warehouse, a trap door hidden in the ground swung up. Three men came out carrying a large, metal-looking object; from my distance it looked like the size of a dresser. If it took three of them to move, then it had to be heavy. They placed it in front of the door and ran back to their hole.

One went back with a helmet that covered his face and thick gloves, holding some sort of equipment. It wasn't until he knelt by the door and sparks began flying that I realized what he was doing. *He's welding it shut?*

I was stunned. I expected General Glaive to stroll in and take down everyone, but I suppose he wasn't bulletproof. Instead of fighting they were trapping them. But what would they do with them after that?

The heavy object held the door in place as he secured it further, and I waited for my question of, "Now what?" to be answered. When Tetchion moved away from the door I heard a small sigh of relief from General Glaive. Instead of using the lights he spoke, "Tyrus, go."

Another trap door swung open from the back of the building. Tyrus climbed out, carrying something like a grenade launcher; I could only guess. He knelt down and aimed it before shooting something through the back window.

"Did he ... just blow people up?" The thought shocked me so much that I questioned the general before thinking about it.

"It's smoke."

The bland answer, without anger or irritation, encouraged me to prod more. "Smoke?"

"To set off the sprinklers."

I knitted my brows. "Are they still working in an abandoned building like this?"

His eyes met mine, and the smooth way he responded gave him an air of an undercover know-it-all, "They do now."

Of course. He was the general. He could have the water turned back on in an old building if he wanted. All he had to do was say the word.

"What good does that do?"

"They won't feel like fighting when we're through." He rose from his place with equipment in hand. "Get up." I stood up.

His next orders were for his men. "Lower the range on the jammer."

He hung the communicator on his belt and pulled out a small phone. Though he didn't say anything, it was clear he sent some sort of message out.

When he moved towards the warehouse, I didn't need any orders to follow. His men dispersed around the building, Dorrius and Tyrus staying on the same side as us.

He stayed so focused on what they were doing

that I jumped when his eyes shot to me. "Why are you here?"

"I heard about the police and I wanted to warn you ..."

"Why were you at the other warehouse?"

I felt a need to cover up my shady business, but Valli was in danger, and the general was here to deal with the gang, right? Breathing became harder as I panicked, both from fear and stress, and the words came out in a confused jumble. "I think my friend has been kidnapped. I haven't been able to find him anywhere. His name is Valli, and he doesn't have anything to do with any of this, he was just following me around because I heard they had the king's necklace. P-please, can you help find him?"

Even though the general was here to deal with the gang, I wasn't sure if he would listen to my request. My single friend probably didn't matter much in a country of over three hundred million, and my plea would sound petty to someone like General Glaive. I clasped my hands together in front of my chest. My whole body felt hot and sweaty; I could only imagine how flushed my face looked.

Only a tiny furrowing of his brows gave any indication he was listening. "Go back home and let us handle this."

My heart sank. He didn't care? I wasn't sure I should have expected more, but I had been hoping. My ears slowly drooped as he didn't seem to have anything else to say to me. I glanced to the other two, but they had no words for me, either.

But Valli wasn't the only one I was worried about. "There's also a whole group of people at the Mosley warehouse. I think they're being held hostage. They need help."

"They will be retrieved when it isn't dangerous to do so." A small pause almost gave me a chance to question him again, but perhaps sensing I would be persistent, he cut me off, "We're dealing with violent criminals. If we're discovered while moving innocent victims they could be caught in the middle of a shoot-out."

Though I tried to work it out in my mind, my thoughts felt numb. Too much had been happening and somewhere along the way I'd blown a fuse.

"Go home," he repeated, his voice lowering a notch, "Don't drink the poison."

While I crept away, I heard a few last words before I was too far.

"Why are we letting him go? He's shady." Tyrus sounded disappointed and baffled. He avoided confronting General Glaive, instead facing Dorrius.

"He clearly came here to help us. We don't want to discourage people from helping us. We didn't need his information this time, but we may next time." I could identify Dorrius's voice by now.

"Listen to Dorrius. He knows what he's talking about," the general confirmed his answer.

A convoy of small trucks whizzed by me before I got more than two hundred yards. I stopped to watch as they pulled up to the side of the warehouse, back ends facing the wall. Tetchion had moved to the same side as General Glaive, and it looked like he was cutting a small hole at the base of the wall, while Tyrus shot more things through the window in the back. *More smoke?*

It didn't take much longer for people to attempt to crawl out through the only opening they could reach, sopping wet and barely even able to fit through. They were grabbed and restrained the moment they showed themselves, and escorted to the back of trucks. It took a moment before I realized the people who had driven the trucks were in pink. *Police?! But they're corrupt!*

Bewildered, I worked it out in my head. One of the trucks was filled and locked up, and I watched it drive away, not in my direction, but towards the capital. Maybe they weren't police from the area. If General Glaive brought his own troops, maybe he had brought police from home as well.

Thinking back on the strategizing from the other night, and now on this, it seemed General Glaive played defensively, and I, fortunately, didn't make his list of priorities.

I left, but I didn't go back to the hotel. Even if I didn't know where Valli was, I knew where some other people who needed help were. The least I could do was tell them that help was coming.

8

Hundreds of years ago Queen Larayan boasted of an extensive and expensive wine collection. When she hired servants she warned them not to drink her wine. Direct orders.

But she never went down to drink or see the wine herself. Two servants who were frustrated with her finally figured that she would never know the difference and they went into the wine cellar to help themselves.

Their bodies were found the next day. All of the wine had been poisoned for any servants who dared to defy her. She was the famous Poison Queen, and although she did questionable things, she was never openly criticized for it. She had told them not to drink the wine, after all.

I knew well the meaning behind Glaive's warning. "Don't drink the poison." It meant, "Do what I say or something bad will happen to you."

I couldn't let myself be scared off. I'd search for Valli until he was found.

On my way back to the second warehouse, the sweatshop, I smelled smoke, but I didn't see anything until the building was in view. Wisps of smoke were beginning to drift towards the sky in front of the door.

Fire! My mind screamed. I sped up. I barely spotted two people leaving but I didn't have the presence of mind to identify them.

Flames climbed up the front of the warehouse and continued to grow. Without thought, I went into a full sprint. Screams erased any hope that everyone had already gotten out.

With the entrance and garage door engulfed in flames, I searched for another way in. There were only the windows, which were too high for them to reach from inside.

I ran to the storage shed to look for something to use. Most of the items were for basic maintenance, but I found a long hose coiled on the ground and grabbed it and the ladder and ran to the window with them.

Digging the ladder into the ground, I climbed up and shoved the window open, breaking one of the hinges in the process. Inside people had scurried towards the back in a panic.

"Over here!" I shouted at them, folding the hose over itself and dropping it through the window. Smoke was filling up the room; I could already feel it stinging my eyes.

At first, my shout seemed to be drowned out by the commotion, but one person nearby scampered towards the window. Shortly thereafter, others began to follow her until a swarm of people poured towards the wall. When the first person started climbing up, I felt the rubber hose stretching, ready to tear at any moment, but people under her started pushing her, relieving some of the pressure.

Once she was close enough, I reached out to pull her up, yanking her out the window. I had no time to be gentle. She hit the ground with a thud and rolled away, coughing.

They kept shoving and lifting to get out as fast as possible. People piled up outside until only one was left. As he was pulling himself up with the hose I felt his weight stretching it again, but there was no one underneath him to hold him up. I held on as tight as I could, willing him to go quicker before the hose broke. He struggled scaling the wall, barely pulling himself up an inch at a time as he tried to get a good grip and find the best position to climb.

It snapped when he neared the top. Feeling it tear just in time, I thrust a hand through the window and grabbed him before he fell. My muscles strained and trembled. Unable to hold him with one arm, I had no choice but to grab him with my other hand, too. It was all I could do to hold him up; without a grip on anything else it was impossible for me to lift him. My chest felt as if the window sill would cut right through it because of the extra weight. I squeezed my eyes shut against the smoke; the heat bit at my skin. I didn't know how much longer I could hold onto him.

Then something grabbed my ankles and pulled on me. Being dragged over the frame grated my skin even through my clothes, but he was partially pulled through before my grip broke from the pressure. I fell back and hit the ground as other people ran up to the building and grabbed him, tugging him through.

Aching all over, I somehow managed to roll over and stumble to my feet. The group had gathered away from the building and I headed to them.

"Is everyone out?" I asked with my arms wrapped around myself, as if they were keeping my body from falling apart.

They glanced at each other but didn't answer. Then it came to me. I didn't see the two little ones. They were probably still in the back room, and all I had left of the hose was a small scrap.

I spun to face the building and felt my chest throb. The fire had engulfed the middle now, with the front half dying down as it moved.

With an arm pasted against my chest I ran to the front of the warehouse. The door where the fire had started was falling apart. Inside, the fire was catching on the boxes and walls.

I took a deep breath and slammed through the door, tripping and falling onto one hand while I covered my nose and mouth with the other. I pushed myself up and darted through the building, swerving to avoid piles of fabric and boxes going up in flames. The heat got to me quickly. Not just in the flames, but in the air, the smoke … My skin was broiling.

Smoke blocked my vision. I maneuvered around the hot spots while barreling forward. In the back I managed to force my eyes open, seeing the door through the tears. I couldn't hold my breath much longer and I knew better than to breathe in the air. As my lungs started fighting me, I fumbled with the door, forcing the knob in until it swung open and I nearly fell.

I slammed my hip against it to close it. The flames hadn't reached this room yet but I could feel the

heat on the door. The two kids were still inside the room; the younger one was crying, arms wrapped around the older one who stared, face pale, fingers digging into the little one's back.

I examined the room. They had the projects they were working on and an old table. I pushed the table over to the back wall and climbed onto it. It bent under my weight.

"Come on!" I rushed them. They followed my lead without question, the older one pulling the younger by the arm. None of us could reach the window on our own. The table shook as they climbed on it. The first looked up at me and the second rubbed his eyes with his sleeve.

"Here." I knelt down, holding out my hands to give one of them a boost.

The older placed his foot in my hands and I lifted him up as high as I could. He grabbed the edge of the window, fitting through easier than I had, but he paused.

"It's really far down."

"It's okay, just jump," I reassured him. He sat on the ledge as he looked down before finally slipping off.

The other was still wiping his eyes when I grabbed him and picked him up. "Hurry, you need to get out the window." He was shorter but just as heavy. I fidgeted with my grip on his feet as he wriggled. The smell of smoke was getting stronger. I shoved him up a little too fast, I figured, since he bumped his head on the window.

"Ow!"

"Sorry. Just get out!" I apologized but it wasn't the time to worry about bumps. With an extra heave, he managed to pull himself up and a wave of relief washed over me when he disappeared on the other side.

Now me. The table didn't get me high enough. I surveyed the room. The kids had again been working on what looked to be a purse. Fabric was all over the floor. I grabbed strips of the material and rolled it up, putting knots in it and tying the makeshift bag on the end as a weight. I swung it in a circle and tried several times to toss it through the window. With a glance back, I saw the flames licking under the door.

Finally the handbag flew through. I had no way to tie the other end to something, I could only hope it would catch on the window and be strong enough to stay put, an almost impossible wish, but the only one I had. When I started tugging on it, something yanked on the other side. I waited, letting material slip through my fingers. After a moment I gave it a tug and it pulled taut.

I wrapped it around my hand and began the difficult climb up. The knots helped, but I didn't have time to put them at good spots. One knot taunted me from just out of reach. My arm felt ready to pop out of its socket because I stretched it so far.

With time running out, I shoved off the wall to try and get a little extra height and barely managed to snag the knot. My second hand slammed onto it and I wrenched myself up and grabbed the edge of the window. Fingers strained to their limits, I fought for a good grip. With my last bit of strength, I dragged myself high enough to throw my arm over the ledge, and I squeezed through face first. I yanked myself through and hit the dirt outside with a thump and a bounce.

I lay there for a moment, catching my breath. My body ached, my eyes stung, my throat and lungs burned. When I turned my eyes up, the older boy was sitting by some old pipes outside the building where the other end of the material had been tied to it.

As I staggered back to my feet, my body was drained of all energy, but everyone was out. I was exhausted and relieved at once.

"Are you okay?" I asked.

He nodded.

I pushed myself forward to check on the others. As soon as I reached the edge of the building I ducked back around the corner. A truck was parked by the group of escapees. The axe wielder stood out from the crowd, with the same woman and man as before. A variety of new people accompanied them. One girl only looked to be about my age and was even shorter than I was. She wore a military-style coat that was black like the Rhodaren army's uniform. It looked like it was a size too large, and her hair was disheveled and hung a few inches below her shoulders.

She pointed, weaving through them as she counted them up, and announced when she was done, "Three are missing. Where are they?"

The group fell silent; some eyes turned the opposite direction from us.

"The two little ones are still inside," one of the hostages answered, his eyes on the ground.

"You." the teenager pointed at one of her gang. "Go round up the one that ran. Start getting them in the truck. We'll take them to Sundecht." He ran off in the direction the group had been glancing while others herded the escapees towards the truck.

The woman, who had accompanied Axe and the other man earlier, spoke up, "We can probably still get the other two out." She took a step towards us.

"Iona!" The teenager stopped her before she got far. "I'm not risking someone valuable for kids who have the potential to be valuable." Then she spun around, gesturing to two of the other members. "You two go check if they're alive." Not a hint of concern in her voice.

I took a step back as the two members approached.

"Hey!" one cried out. "There's someone back there!"

I stumbled back, turning around to get the kids.

"What?" It was the teenager's voice again, sounding momentarily confused before giving another command, "Axe, go get them."

With one last glance back, I saw the group of escapees being herded into the truck and the huge woman heading our way. I gathered the two kids, waving wildly for them to start moving. I guided them around the corner to keep out of view as long as possible before grabbing each of them by the hand. We ran across the open field, crushing dried weeds under our feet.

By the time we reached the brush my lungs were attempting to explode. The nine-year-old stumbled and I barely kept him from falling to the ground. As much as I willed myself to keep going, my legs were numb and I wanted to vomit. My sprint turned into a shuffle. My lungs were so dried out that I was sure they'd shriveled up into raisins.

"We need to hide somewhere," I told them. I searched for anywhere we could conceal ourselves without being spotted, but none of the vegetation was large enough.

Finally, one of my legs gave out and I fell onto a knee, stopping the kids. I pulled my arm away from the little one and coughed into it while I struggled to get back up.

Even when I heard the crunch of footsteps getting closer, my body fought me. I forced myself up, turning to face the horned figure nearing us.

"Get behind me." I held my arms out in front of the kids. Something had a stranglehold on my brain and was beating it against the wall. I couldn't get a clear thought out. *What should I tell them to do?*

She slowed when she was only a few yards away, axe in hand. I felt something dry and coarse being pressed into my hand. Not daring to turn away, I caught only a glimpse of the nine-year-old giving me the stick. *Maybe I can jab her in the eye before I'm hacked to pieces.*

Just a yard away she stopped, wordless, looking down at us. Small hands clamped onto one of my arms;

it made me all the more aware of how much I was shaking. She sneered down at me with strangely distant eyes. An eternity passed as I waited for the blow.

Then, without saying a thing, she turned and walked away. I stood in place like a statue, waiting for her to suddenly swivel back around and swing the axe as soon as I turned my back, but the farther away she got, the more my mind began working again. I reached for the kids' hands and began walking away.

"We have to get somewhere safe." I strained my voice to get the words out. One thought began repeating itself in my mind: *water.*

"We can go to my house," the littlest one said.

"Your house?" I repeated.

He nodded with an affirmative, "Nn."

With no time to be picky I agreed, "Okay, where is it?"

"It's the first one that starts with 's.'"

I nodded. Though he didn't seem to know the name of the street I could easily look it up when we got into the city.

The walk back dragged as much as I did. As long as we weren't being chased, I didn't want to push my body beyond its limits. I already had a series of scrapes along my upper torso and my mouth and throat were more parched than I'd ever felt before. When we stumbled back into town, I took a turn into the first shop we came across, buying some water and explaining that there was a fire to the clerk so that she could call for the fire fighters.

113

"Are you sure you're all right? If you breathed in smoke you should go to the hospital."

I ran it through my mind. If I went to the hospital where would the kids end up? General Glaive had said everything here was corrupt. They could end up somewhere bad again.

"I'm fine. I just ran a long way," I assured her.

I downed my entire glass of water in one gulp. The two kids sipped at theirs but didn't seem as affected by the smoke as I was. After a short rest, I ushered them along again.

"All right, we'll get to your house now," I told them, heading to the nearest access panel to look it up. *Sandberry. Probably named after what grows there.*

After boarding a cart and arriving at the street the little one pulled away from me and I followed. On the way he plucked a few reddish berries covered in little brown speckles off some bushes and popped them in his mouth. He led us back to a house – it looked a bit run down, but otherwise fine.

I knocked on the door but he passed me and opened it up, going inside.

"The door isn't locked?" I asked.

I stepped inside the house and investigated as I felt the other boy brush passed me. All of the lights were off and random objects were strewn all over – utensils left on the table, blankets on the ground, scissors on the floor ... It looked abandoned. Marks covered the walls as if someone had been cutting into them, but we were the only ones making any noise.

"Where are your parents?"

"Mom is gone," the younger answered while he browsed through the kitchen.

"Then who lives here?"

"I do." He pointed at himself, and then the other child. "And Loren does. I said he could live here."

"By yourselves?"

I flipped a switch, but the lights didn't come on. I had no more luck with the sink. Everything was shut off.

"How do you get by?"

"He gets the food." The older one indicated the younger. "And I take care of the house."

I glanced around. Although it was dirty for a normal house, it was surprisingly clean for two kids.

I turned to Loren. "What about your parents?"

He quieted momentarily before answering, eyes cast down, "… They died."

"I'm sorry." I furrowed my brows. I hadn't been prepared to take this all in, assuming that they'd been taken from their families. "Someone should be taking care of you two. Especially him."

Loren shook his head. "I can take care of him. We are married." He gestured towards a raggedy little tassel hanging from his left hip. "Merrian made this for me."

There were so many things wrong with that, I didn't even know where to start. They were much too young. Married people had matching tassels, not just one, and it was supposed to be worn on the right side. Those things hardly seemed important enough to argue about here, though.

I watched them putter around the house, using stools to reach things. For their age, they seemed competent, but I was alarmed when the younger one suddenly pulled a knife out from the kitchen. I watched him carry it over to the table, climb on a chair, and start carving into the table top.

"What are you doing?" I ran over and grabbed the knife.

He hung onto it. "I'm drawing!"

"You shouldn't play with knives, you'll cut yourself!" I scolded him as I tried to take it.

"But I do this lots!"

Overpowering him, I pried the knife out of his hand and held it out of his reach. He pouted, jumping down from his chair and stomping away.

I looked after him before turning my attention back to Loren.

"Didn't you say something about a mansion?" I asked. *Perhaps I could drop them off there.*

He busied himself folding blankets on the ground, answering while he concentrated, "Yeah, it's where I used to live."

"All right. I could take you both there; it should have running water and electricity," I offered.

"I don't want to go back," he whined, looking up at me with a pinched expression.

"It'll be safer than here. Where is it?" I took a step towards him but he bolted for the kitchen area, grabbing a knife off the counter and pointing it towards me.

"I don't want to go back!" he yelled. I threw my hands up. Even if I could overwhelm him I didn't want to. Something was wrong.

"Okay," I gave in. "Okay. We won't go there." I kept my voice even, "But it's dangerous to stay here. You guys could be taken again. We need to go somewhere safe. I have a hotel room – it's warm and has running water," I bargained with him, "and no one will know you're there."

He fidgeted, the knife wobbly in his hands, glaring at me before demanding, "You promise?"

I nodded. "I promise. You'll be safe there until we can find someplace for you two."

His hands lowered and he looked away.

I waved him towards me. "Come on. We'll get Merrian and go."

The smaller child needed no convincing to go. With a simple, "Let's go," we were off.

We grabbed an assortment of sweet breads and juices from the bakery on the way back to the hotel, where I took them up to the room. Dropping the food on the table, the first chance I got, I went to the bed and collapsed.

I rolled my head to the side and watched the kids dig into the sweet bread. Merrian poured more powdered sugar on top of it than he could ever need. As long as they were happy and safe for now, I didn't care.

From my spot, I used my entire arm to point as I explained the room to them.

"There's a bathroom there and a bath there. There's a kitchen but you shouldn't try to cook anything on your own. Just get water or something if you need it. And you can use the second bed if you need to."

The second bed. My heart sunk lower than my body. *Valli is still out there. How can I search for him now?*

If I was going to keep looking for Valli, I needed help, but who could I go to? I didn't know anyone in the area. Ellora was too far away to be of any help, and I didn't want to talk to her about my problems. My dad was thousands of miles away as well.

I pushed up onto my elbows. *Dad might be my best option.* He couldn't be here but he could call and I trusted him. The biggest problem would be convincing him not to call the authorities.

I allowed myself a few more minutes to rest before wrestling my body over to the phone. *How am I going to explain this?* I had no idea but I needed to do something. I called Dad.

"Leander?"

"Hi Dad," I jabbered. "I don't have a lot of time to explain but I found these two kids and they don't have anyone to take care of them, and they're here, and they're safe, but I can't stay to watch them. Do you think you could keep calling and checking to make sure they're okay?"

He gazed at me blankly, taking a moment to reply, "Um ... Leander, if they don't have anyone to take care of them, you should call child services."

"No." I waved my hands. "No, the authorities

around here are corrupt." He arched an eyebrow as I babbled, "Please, you have to trust me. They were in a bad situation and I don't want them to end up back there. General Glaive and his men are in the area, so if I can get a note to them, I think I can get them somewhere safe."

He eyed me skeptically, arms folded.

"*Please* Dad, trust me," I begged him.

He was hesitant in his response, but finally answered, "All right, Leander. But you need to get in contact with the proper authorities as soon as possible."

"I will." I nodded, waving the kids over. Merrian had powdered sugar covering his hands and a huge chunk of bread stuffed in his cheek, while Loren had washed his hands and tidied up. "This is Loren and that's Merrian." I turned to them. "This is my dad. He's going to call in and check in on you guys, so just answer the phone when he calls."

"All right," Loren agreed.

"Hello," my dad greeted them awkwardly.

Loren raised a hand halfway. "Hi."

Merrian mumbled something unintelligible.

"All right." I backed away. "You two just stay here. You'll be safe. I'll be back later, okay?" I held a hand up, gesturing for them to stay in place. "Just. Stay safe." I looked to my dad, mumbling, "I love you, Dad."

"I love you, too, Leander."

I inched out of the room, closing the door behind me. I had to trust Dad now. They would be okay.

Fighting the urge to rush, I instead tried to formulate a plan as I walked. I couldn't push myself too hard, not when my body was still recovering. When I left Valli behind, only Axe and I were there. If I could question her somehow maybe I would find out where he was, but how could I do that without ending up dead?

I might need to spy on them for a while, and investigate their other warehouses. I stopped at the entrance of the hotel and leaned on the door frame for a moment, taking several deep breaths and letting out a few coughs.

At the fire, their leader had mentioned some other spot. They seemed to be infesting the entire outlying region, taking over abandoned buildings for their own purposes. When I stopped by the access panel this time, I looked up all of the abandoned buildings I could find on the outskirts of town.

I knew one had burned down, and seen another used to store counterfeit goods. Several others were scattered around. I went over the map until I had memorized it, keeping in mind the locations. Not all of them were named anymore.

It wasn't likely that Axe would be there, though. I needed to find her.

Another place was situated near the middle of them all. It could be a convenient place for them to gather.

Keeping it all in mind, I made the long trek back and headed to the middle warehouse. Something had to be there.

9

When I got to the warehouse, no one else seemed to be around which gave me an opportunity to snoop.

I opened the door slowly to peek before I snuck in. Familiar crates were stacked inside. I didn't see anyone, so I went in. I didn't know what to look for. Anything that could lead me to Valli, or a good hiding spot where I could spy on them when they came back.

After searching the room, I hadn't found anything that stuck out until I noticed a large vent. At first I didn't understand why it caught my eye. Then I figured out what was odd: there seemed to be a light inside of it. There was no grate covering it, and when I climbed up the boxes in front of it to look further I saw a cloth hanging over the other end, with light leaking through.

It was too odd of a place for light for it to be meaningless. Something had to be back there. I squeezed into the vent, thankful again for my small size, and made my way through to the other side expecting to find some sort of hidden stash.

When I poked out the other side I was in a small room with a little girl in the corner. I froze, flustered. Whoever she was, she was in here alone and staring at me confused. I guessed she was around seven.

She had fabric in her hand and was sewing. The white garment she was constructing looked vaguely familiar but I couldn't pinpoint where from.

"Ah ... hi?" I tried not to sound awkward and failed.

"Hi," she responded, still surprised. "Are you a new guy?"

I snatched up the excuse she provided. "Yeah."

I pulled myself all the way into the room, until the cloth dropped behind me to block the light from going out, and tried to start a friendly conversation. "So, what are you doing in here?"

"Just working," she answered. I noticed several differences between her and the people I'd seen before. One, she was here alone. Two, she wasn't locked inside. Three, she didn't look underfed at all. The room was well lit and she had her own personal little work station set up. There was an entirely different feel to the place.

"What are you making?" I examined it. Pink diamonds were pasted in a V-shape under the high collar.

"This." she held up a picture happily. When I saw it I remembered where I'd seen it before. It was what King Lariat wore when he was coronated. The white and pink were strong but not as bold as the soldier's white and reds, giving him a powerful, yet soft, appearance.

She was making a counterfeit. Though it looked impressive for a girl of her age, it wouldn't compare to the real thing.

"It looks good," I said with a half-hearted smile. "So who are you?" *Hopefully my question won't give me away.*

"I'm Kelsy," she answered in a friendly manner. "Who are you?"

"Leander." I figured there was no harm using my real name. She didn't seem dangerous. "So why are you here?"

"It's my safe spot. So no one will find me when everyone is out."

"Oh." I sat down across from her, feeling cramped in the small room with the low ceiling. "And how old are you?"

"I just turned eight," she boasted.

She seemed a little short for eight. "Eight, huh? And you sew?"

"I've been sewing a long time now." She puffed out her chest. "I'm really good at it. I'm going to be a tailor for the king one day."

"Is that so?" I humored her. "Do you need any help?"

She looked up at me, eyes wide.

"No one ever helps me."

Then she pushed aside piles of fabric to make room, sitting on her knees on the other side of the splayed-out garment. Her round face looked cute when she smiled. It was framed by her bob haircut, which also accentuated her snub nose that turned up slightly at the tip.

She plopped down on her stomach and kicked her legs as she demonstrated putting on a jewel for me. "We have to get the jewels on like this."

She grabbed a jewel out of her pile and glued it on around the neckline. I lugged myself over to the spot she made and picked up one of the jewels, looking at the picture. I tried to place it evenly with the others. I was impressed with how well she'd managed to imitate the original.

"So, has anyone else new been around here?" I asked.

"Not really."

I wasn't sure what else I was expecting from someone tucked in a hideaway.

A thud on the wall resounded inside the room and made my heart do a somersault. It was followed by a shout. "Kelsy. Food. Come on."

"Okay, coming!" She got up to run over to the vent opening. The room was big enough for her to stand.

"I'm just working with ..." The panic was clear on my face as I flailed my arms to signal her to stop. Her smile disappeared as she looked at me and continued in a weaker voice, "... with my stuff."

She pushed the flap aside and crawled out.

I peeked out. Just as I thought, Axe was there. Some food was set out using a crate as a table and another as a chair. Her axe was still strapped to her back but the helmet was off, revealing a mess of tangled, shoulder-length hair. She pulled her gloves off and set them to the side. The little girl climbed down and hopped over, sitting across from her.

"How did everything go?" Kelsy asked.

"We got it settled," Axe answered simply.

I came all this way hoping for an opportunity to eavesdrop on her and now all I wanted to do was get away from her. I settled down near the end of the vent, focusing on my goal. Even though it felt like an eternity, Valli had only disappeared two days before. It was possible she'd mention it.

They ate in silence. Other people began drifting into the warehouse, starting with the teenager from earlier. She was speaking over her shoulder to the woman she'd called Iona. The man who had accompanied Iona and Axe walked in behind them.

"I knew he did something to the Mosley when he left me a message. The old man is too predictable. We wouldn't get anywhere if I let him take charge," she scoffed at the idea as she brushed back strands of hair that had fallen in front of her face.

The man spoke, his voice tense, "But he's got a lot more people."

"Pah!" the teen spat back. "Useless idiots. They think they're tough when they get a gun in their hands." She gestured towards Axe. "Axe could plow through a dozen of them by herself."

Axe didn't turn her head when she glanced back, remaining focused on her meal. She had an oval face with thin eyebrows, a long nose and thick lips. Despite the messy hair I could see people finding her handsome and being interested in her, if it weren't for the part about her being a murderer putting a damper on things. Kelsy stuffed a large piece of meat in her mouth with her bare hands.

"You really think you can win?" the man asked.

"Of course I can." She swung around to face him taking one aggressive step towards him, her hand pointing in his face. "I'm going to pay him a visit to discuss that little fire he set." With that she shrugged, flinging her arms out with a self-assured smirk. "I'll take care of him then."

"I'm done," Kelsy announced, hopping off her box. "I'm going to finish the gown."

Before she could get far, Axe called after her, "Wash your hands, first."

The man stepped by her with a huff as the girl ran across the room, placing his hands on his hips. "That's pretty cold, putting your own sister to work."

Axe shrugged. "She *likes* doing that sort of thing."

The teenager headed out of view with the man following. Iona started in their direction but stopped and spun on her heel, looking to Axe, who was quietly eating. Her ponytail whisked over her shoulder to her back.

"How are you doing?" she asked, hand on her hip as she leaned over. Even when Axe was sitting down, it wasn't necessary for Iona to lean over.

Axe shrugged, answering in a monotone voice, "Just a little bruised."

"It's a good thing you always wear a lot of padding." Iona raised a hand to her cheek, bemused smile on her lips.

"Nn," Axe grunted back. "I just got nicked by the truck. I'm fine." Her attention went back to her food, head turned away from Iona.

"You have that serious face on again," Iona said with a devious grin. Axe glanced at her from the corner of her eye. Iona kept going without a hitch, "I had a bird earlier, too, because it was cheep."

Axe quirked a brow at her before letting out a loud laugh. Iona twirled around again to keep going. The laughter died as quickly as it had come and Axe shook her head as if to rid herself of the cheer, but a small grin still clung to her face.

Then Kelsy returned and climbed back into the vent. I backed up into the small room. When she got all the way in, she stood up with hands on her hips and a stern expression, looking down at me, but spoke quietly enough to not be heard outside, "Who are you?"

I gazed up at her, not certain how to respond.

"I'll tell Sissy!" she warned me.

I threw my hands up, trying to settle her down. "No, no! I'm not here for anything bad, honest. I'm just looking for a friend of mine."

"Hmm?"

"He disappeared a few days ago and I think he might have been taken. He's about my height, hair down to his waist, on the pretty side … He was hurt the last time I saw him and I need to get him to a hospital. Have you seen him?"

She put a finger to her lip, her eyes turning towards the ceiling for a minute before shaking her head. Somehow my heart sank even though I had convinced myself not to get my hopes up.

"He's a really nice guy; he just ended up at the wrong place at the wrong time. I had to leave him for a bit at the warehouse closer to the city, and when I came back he was gone. Can you help me find him?" I pleaded with her.

"Um ..." She tilted her head, then smiled. "Yeah, okay."

"Can you think of any place he might be?"

She pursed her lips and furrowed her brows for a moment before perking back up and announcing, "I'll ask Sissy!"

My insides leapt, but she scurried out of the vent before I could stop her. I lay at the end of the vent, body tense as I listened.

"Sissy," she called out as she hopped down on the boxes. Axe was wiping her hands off, giving her a passing look. "You were at that place the other day, close to the city. Did anything happen?"

She tossed her dirtied rag to the side of the box and leaned forward, frowning. "Not really. Just normal business."

"Did you meet anyone?"

"Just the regular people."

The tension in my body faded and I became slack. *So she doesn't tell her about anything?* I was both relieved and disappointed, relieved that the eight-year-old was spared the details of what happened and disappointed that she probably wouldn't be able to get any information about Valli. I wanted to hop out and shake Axe until she coughed up what happened – if only it wouldn't end in me being hacked to pieces.

"Okay." Kelsy accepted her answer with calm cheer, pulling herself back up into the vent and coming back.

When she came back in, she sat on her knees and said, "She doesn't know."

I let myself exhale, leaning against the wall. "Is this the only place you're ever at?"

She held a hand up to her mouth and giggled with an emphatic, "No!" Then, as she mulled it over, she turned her eyes to the ceiling. "We have lots of places. Like warehouses, and factories ... And storage places and stuff!"

"And you've been to them?" I perked an ear up.

"Mhmm." she nodded.

"Do you think you could tell me about them? It might help me find him."

"Mm, okay." She shifted to sit on her butt with her legs out and leaned back on her arms. "Well, there's a factory. Lots of stuff happens there."

"You think he might be there?"

"I don't know. Maybe. People go there a lot." She shrugged.

It was better than nothing. I could at least see what was there. "Where is it?"

"Well, it's, um ..." She waved an arm. "It's that way somewhere. There's a vent close to the ground on one side, but it's not really a vent. You can just go inside if you take it off."

I scrounged through the map in my mind for a factory in that direction. I did recall a large building, but I didn't know what it was when I was looking at the map.

"All right," I said, resolved to give it a look at least. "I just have to figure out how to sneak out of here so I can take a look."

"You can use the secret exit," she offered.

"There's a secret exit?" I gaped.

"Yeah." She stood up and took three quick steps, pulling up a piece of the floor. "In case I ever need to get out."

I crawled over to her and examined the hole. I could only see far enough to tell that it was a crude tunnel. *It won't be the first crude tunnel I've been in.*

I threw my legs over the side, ready to drop in, before looking back at her. "Thanks."

She smiled brightly in response. "Uh-huh."

I pushed off the edge and landed at the bottom. The tunnel wasn't large enough for me to stand up straight. I hunched over and crawled through much of it, going much farther than I expected before reaching an end.

Shoving a trap door up, I crawled out onto the ground. Withered plants surrounded me. I saw the warehouse in the distance behind me.

I climbed to my feet and made my way to the factory.

10

My lungs were prepared to eject themselves. After arriving, I saw a man guarding the front door of the factory. I was lucky he didn't hear me gasping for air. Moments later, two trucks pulled up. Iona and Axe got out of one; the teenage leader and the guy came out of the other.

The guard at the door pointed his pistol at them as they approached with the leader in front. She held up her empty hands as she came near him, but he didn't lower the gun.

"If it isn't the little princess ..." he sneered.

"Don't talk down to me," she answered coolly, coming within his reach with her hands still up. In a flash she balled up a fist and jabbed him in the stomach. When he keeled over, she grabbed the back of his neck and shoved him to the ground. "I'm the queen. Axe."

She gestured towards the man on the ground with a slight bow. Axe grabbed him by the scruff and the seat of his pants, picking him up before ramming the door several times. As soon as it broke open she threw him at a few of the people standing inside, and her group made their way into the building.

I probably won't find anything about Valli here. I eyed the side of the building. *Something is going on here. General Glaive was interested in information. Maybe if I find some other information I could get him to help me find Valli.*

The thought passed through my head and I immediately shook it away. *No, I won't do that. If I find out something, I may be able to help free those people. I can't try to bribe them.*

I inched towards the building. Kelsy had made it sound easy to sneak in, but I didn't know my way around like she did.

The grate at the base of the wall was much smaller than I'd imagined it. I jiggled it around and pulled it off, flattening myself on the ground to squeeze through. *This is probably a lot easier for Kelsy.*

The sounds of a skirmish resounded in the distance but didn't seem to be coming in my direction. I brushed off my aching front side. Wriggling around on the ground hadn't helped make it feel better after being scraped up by the window sill. Bits of leaves and dirt fluttered to the ground when I stood.

I was in awe of the size of the factory. Stairs led up to catwalk overhead. Defunct conveyor belts were all over, and gigantic tanks, twenty or so feet tall, stood next to me. It was a maze of unfamiliar machinery. *I'll have to look up what they used to make here.* Cranes that traveled along beams covered the ceiling.

Sounds echoed through the factory, making it hard to tell where they were coming from. Grunts, yells, screams, a few shots. I carefully made my way up the stairs to get a better view.

When I got to the top, I crawled, positioning myself under a control panel to keep hidden as well as I could. About a dozen people were in the center of the factory, no one I recognized.

The teenager made her way to the center with Iona and the man hanging back. I didn't see Axe, but I did hear more fighting in the background.

"Signe," a middle-aged man stepped out of the group and addressed her.

"I got your message." She stopped a couple of yards away from him, chin held high despite her small stature.

"You forced my hand, killing some of my people."

"You touched the Mosley." She shrugged, holding her entire arms out to the side as she did with a smirk. "I couldn't allow that." Her grin was too wide, eyes too large. I imagined waking up to her would be much like waking up to a room full of dolls all staring at me.

"I'm surprised you're in such a good mood."

"I didn't lose much. Just two pipsqueaks and materials." Her smile widened and her voice lowered, "You know I have plenty more than that."

His expression turned grim. Signe took long steps, moving in a circle. He stayed across from her, matching her movement with smaller steps.

"We have bigger concerns than just making money right now," he said. "General Glaive is here. We need to avoid drawing attention to ourselves. One of the warehouses was razed to the ground, and I don't think it was you who did it."

"So you want to lay low and hope he forgets about us?" she spat it out with a disgusted look on her face. "This is why we wouldn't get anywhere if you were in charge."

He narrowed his eyes. "You're too young to be leader, Signe. No one wants to follow a seventeen-year-old."

"I have plenty enough people following me, and they're of better quality than yours." She flicked an ear, glancing towards the entrance from the corner of her eye. "It doesn't sound like yours are putting up much of a fight."

"I wonder how pure her attentions are in following you."

At that, Signe let out a brazen laugh, mocking him, "It's cute that you think anyone here has pure intentions. I couldn't care less what her intentions are, as long as she gets the job done."

"Regardless," he spoke louder, "we'll be inviting our own deaths if we keep this up. We need to wait until the general leaves."

"He's alone with a few men. It's a simple matter of getting rid of them," she jeered.

The other man looked aghast, reeling back. "You can't simply kill the general."

"Oh, is he immune to bullets?" She stopped stalking him, and he stopped across from her. "Cower in a hole all you want. I'll handle things. Then," she leered at him, "it's back to business."

He pursed his lips. "If you assassinate the general, the government will retaliate in full. It may be good for other criminals, but it will be the end of us."

"Don't be so sure of that." She leaned in. "From what I understand the nobles don't care much for him.

He's stirring things up, acting like a tank on the blitz and keeping them from getting more money and resources from the king." She waved her hand dismissively. "If he's gone they'll put on a big show of being devastated, but inside they'll be relieved."

"You can't be serious. This is akin to killing the king himself. Whether they like him or not the government will have to find the people responsible."

"Aren't they already after us?" She gave him a cocky smile. "People are fickle. It'll be a travesty until it's not."

"He's the general!"

"So what? We have a spare."

"I didn't work with your mother for two decades to have the entire nation after us."

"My mother didn't build this whole operation up from scratch so that you could lie back and get rich off her legacy." She pointed at him, the smile disappearing for a second. "We have ten thousand people, and I intend to make it even bigger. We'll be a force that can take on the army itself!"

"How do you plan on doing that? Certainly we have a nice, steady business, but it takes money and resources to expand."

"I have plenty of assets." She took a step towards him. "I'm sure you've heard about the necklace."

His feet stayed in place although he turned his head away, as though he wanted to move back. "I've heard rumors."

She continued towards him, getting in his face

and pulling a small box out of her coat. She popped it open, revealing a brilliant chandelier necklace.

"See for yourself. Go ahead, look it over," she urged him.

He hesitated to reach for it, but when he picked it up he examined it quizzically.

"You'll see that it's no fake. We have paperwork for it." She smirked. "That little necklace is worth more than everything you have."

He looked front and back. "It certainly looks real."

"Put it back in," she barked at him, smile vanishing. It was replaced by a frightening glower that radiated with anger like I'd never seen before.

He set the necklace down in the box and she snapped it shut almost fast enough to take off a finger. She tucked the box back into her coat. Her smirk re-emerged, but that brief glare was burned into my mind.

"I'll have the whole outfit soon. And then I'll be making *real* money."

"If you want to risk your life then I won't stop you. But I'll be waiting things out."

The grin didn't leave her face, but finally she stepped back with a shrug and a shake of her head. "Have it your way."

She turned to leave. As she went, the other two fell in line behind her.

She plans on killing General Glaive. I have to warn him! Frightening or not, I couldn't let something happen to him. I needed to find him.

I crept back down the stairs and squeezed out of the factory, carefully sneaking away until I was a safe distance from the factory.

The general could be anywhere and I had a limited amount of time to find him.

11

I didn't know where to start looking for the general. I spent the day running around town, asking people if they'd seen or heard anything. No one had a clue where he'd gone and there were no signs of him at the town hall. *He may be doing something outside of the city, but where?*

After several wasted hours, I decided to check back at the hotel to bring the kids some more food and drinks. I went in carrying a basket of goodies and saw people chatting in stunned voices at the front desk. I ignored them as I passed until I heard, "I wonder if that means General Oske is going to be in charge again."

I backtracked to the desk and butted in, "Did something happen?"

"General Glaive is in the hospital," the receptionist readily divulged the information. "Apparently he's been seriously injured. It's on the news."

I left them to their conversation and ran up to my room as fast as I could. I tossed the basket onto the counter and dove towards the v-phone, pulling up the news. Sure enough, General Glaive had been shot and was in critical condition in the hospital. It was surreal. Even if I didn't find him, I thought it would be prevented somehow.

I should have looked harder. Maybe I should have looked somewhere else. Why did I even go to the town hall? I only saw him there once.

My mind reeled from the shock. I don't know where it went, but my blood got marching orders and beat a hasty retreat from my face. Perhaps it was all going to my stomach because I felt like puking.

At that moment, the v-phone rang. My dad's information showed on the menu and I answered right away despite feeling sick.

"Oh, Leander, you're there." He sounded surprised, and then worried. "Are you okay?"

"I just heard the news about General Glaive," I explained.

"What news?"

I fell into a stunned silence. I thought he'd have heard fast since he was in the army. "He's ... been shot. He's critically injured in a hospital here."

"Oh." His eyes narrowed and he frowned. "Are you sure? I haven't heard anything about that."

"It's on the news."

I slumped back in the chair. *Now what?* The sound of the kids fussing over the food irritated my ears.

"I'll have to talk to the other guys about this," my dad said as his eyes wandered away from the video.

"Dad!" I called for him suddenly. "Wait. I ... I may not be able to get a message to General Glaive, but his men should be around the hospital, right? I could always tell them about these kids, at least."

He looked back at me silently.

"Just keep checking on them for a bit longer, okay? I'm going to try."

"Be careful, Leander," he warned me.

I didn't even bother hanging up before scurrying around to gather writing materials. Plopping down at the desk, I started writing a note. I put down everything I could think of: their names, the hotel, the room number, and a short explanation. I folded it so quickly and messily that I may as well have crumpled it up and shoved it in my pocket, and then I was off again.

Looking for the hospital that General Glaive was in was a much easier feat. The city had a limited number of hospitals, and I could only picture him using the most renowned one, that is, the one that Valli had come here for.

When I showed up, I was recognized by some of the staff. That allowed me some freedom to move without question. I tried my best not to look lost as I maneuvered around the halls. Sneaking around the hospital reminded me of being in Wilten Crags and sent a shudder through me. *This is not that hospital,* I reminded myself.

I jumped when I spotted a uniform at the end of one of the hallways. Only one. Tyrus. I approached with caution.

He spotted me well before I got to him, watching me with his head tilted back and raised brows. He said nothing, even when I stood in front of him. Uncomfortable, I dug out the note and held it up.

He gave it a critical look, with his lip twitching

up in the corner as he accepted it. "A love letter for me?"

"No!" I bristled. "It's for Dorrius!"

"A love letter for Dorrius?" he corrected himself.

"It's not a love letter!" I felt myself flushing. At least I found that blood I'd misplaced earlier.

He began straightening it to read it.

"I said it was for Dorrius!"

"Personal notes are against the rules," he answered, eyes gleaming, not slowing down. "Your hotel and room number?" he questioned me with a wry smirk.

"I told you it's not a love letter!" I started overheating, and tried to change the subject in a more somber tone, "Is General Glaive okay?"

The smirk didn't leave his face when he glanced down at me, and he responded in disturbingly good humor, "As well as anyone can be when they're shot in the head." He placed a finger to the side of his head and imitated an explosion sound.

I stared at him, aghast. *How can he say something like that with a smile? About his own boss?*

I glanced around him to the doors at the end of the hallway, wishing that I could see through walls.

"If you try to get in there I'll have to kill you," he warned me with the same amused grin.

I took a step back. The way he grinned at me scared me and I ran away before he could say anything else. Tyrus and I might have similar scores and looks, but I was nothing like him. All I could do was hope the message got passed on to Dorrius.

I stood outside the hospital entrance with my hands in my pockets, my eyes scouring the streets. *What now?* For the time being I had done what I could to get the kids somewhere safe. I tried to warn General Glaive, but I failed. Now who would save the hostages? General Oske was still at the castle and I doubted he was going to come here. Would the Melechtions continue pursuing the case without their leader?

I paced around the front of the hospital. *The kids are safe at the hotel. Should I go try to get the hostages out?* Signe's brazen actions worried me. What would she do next? She discussed wanting to expand. I could only imagine how bad things would get then.

I stared at the ground, lost in thought. I couldn't just go home and do nothing, could I? They had been fine with me providing information before. Maybe if I could at least bring something to the Melechtions they would still do something.

The thought of meeting Tyrus at the hospital again made me shudder. *Where are the others anyway? In the room with General Glaive?*

I brushed aside the useless thought and finally made use of my legs, heading for the nearest cart. Information it was. I'd at least find the hostages and report back. *And who better to ask than Kelsy?*

I made my way back to the warehouse where I'd met Kelsy. The biggest difference I noticed was a familiar truck inside the building with a partially crushed front corner. Again the place was empty, and I made my way into the vent.

She looked surprised to see me again, but smiled widely. I noted the outfit she was making was getting closer to completion.

"Hi," I greeted her.

"Hi! Are you going to help out again?"

"No, I don't think so. I ... still haven't found my friend, and I had some more questions." I sat down and crossed my legs. "Do you know a lot about the different warehouses your, uh, group owns? Like where they make outfits like that?"

"A little bit, but I usually don't go to those. I make my stuff here." She gestured around the room.

The horrible thought came to the front of my mind, *There's more than one.*

"Can you tell me where they are at least? All the ones you know?"

"Well, um ..." she began listing them as I marked them off on the map in my head.

I nodded at her when she finished. "Thanks. That helps a lot."

She smiled with a giggle in response, scrunching her nose.

I turned to leave but she stopped me. "Did you see what I did?"

When I turned my head she was holding up the pants to go with the outfit, half sewn.

"Yeah, it looks good," I told her with a half-hearted smile. She beamed.

I began crawling through the vent when I heard the door open and stopped, ducking back out of view.

Signe strutted into the warehouse accompanied by the man she used as a driver. They were in the middle of a conversation when they came in.

"… long day. We need to gather everyone up. Axe can handle the people who have a problem with the change."

The man responded, concerned, "I'm not sure we can rely on her."

"Don't worry about her, I've got her under control," she answered confidently.

"How can you be sure?"

"She follows Iona around like feces clinging to a fish." Her lips curled into a grin. "Besides, I know her secret."

"She's a cold-blooded murderer. What can you possibly know about her that she cares about?" He threw out his arms, almost yelling.

She whipped around to face him, causing him to stumble back.

"That's none of your concern. Just do your job and I'll handle her," she spat out. "Now clean up that truck!"

"I've been working on it," he muttered exasperated, but with reservation. "There's puke everywhere."

"I don't care, it's still valuable. Get to it." She pointed at the truck.

He grabbed a rag and slunk over to the damaged vehicle, climbing into the passenger side. I backed out of the vent.

"Do you know where they've gone recently?" I whispered to Kelsy.

"I think they went to the Mosley the other day, and they went to the one that's south of here, and they went to the factory, and ... um ..."

"Is the south one called 'Sundecht'?"

"I think so."

I figured I had the information I needed. "I think that's enough. Thanks. I'm going to take the secret way out."

"Okay!"

On my way out, I plotted. That southern warehouse probably held the hostages and Axe had some sort of secret. First, I'd find the hostages, then see if I could figure out the secret and report back to the Melechtion group. Any of them but Tyrus. He made my skin crawl.

I made the trek to the other warehouse -- a bland rectangle building with stark, gray walls and familiar tiny windows. A hefty lock hung on the front door confirmed my theory. People were locked inside.

Carting around an old scaffold, I built my way up to the window. I only found one plank, so I set it up as high as I could and climbed up the metal bars to get to it. The window led to a small, empty room in the back.

This would be trickier than I thought. I'd need to go inside to talk to them. I started gathering everything I could find – boxes, pieces of wood, broken equipment – and shoving it through the window until I thought I could build a decent escape.

I dropped down. Looking over the stuff in the room, I began pushing it around, stacking boxes then putting some pieces of wood across them. It wasn't great but it would do. I'd worry about it later. I headed farther into the building.

More people than I imagined were inside. They must have combined two warehouses. I recognized some and didn't recognize others.

Not seeing any gang members there, I announced my presence to them, "Hey." I received some stares, many confused.

"I wanted to let you guys know, General G ... The Melechtions are working on getting you free," I told them.

"I heard the general was dead," a voice cried out from the crowd.

"I ..." I paused. "I'm not sure about his condition, but the Melechtions are still here. I don't think they'd quit."

The hope I'd wanted to give them didn't carry over. Doubt clouded their faces as they continued about their work. I spotted the woman who had explained about Axe before. Even though I was beginning to share their feelings of despair, I refused to give up.

"Umm, can I talk to you?" I approached her cautiously.

Her eyes snapped my way. "About what?" She didn't have the same sharpness in her voice as last time.

"Axe. You knew about her before. Do you know

about any secrets she has?"

"Secrets?" she asked.

"Well, I don't know, do you know her name?"

"I didn't know her like that before. We were stuck in the same place for a while, but we never really talked," she explained.

"I've never heard anyone use her name. Could it be something she's hiding?"

A frown creased her face. "Not likely. I just didn't know her, but I doubt she's ever hid it. People started calling her Axe because ... Do I really need to explain that? She only ever really stood out because of her size."

"Her size?" I furrowed my brows. It was hard to picture any of the hostages being large when they looked so underfed.

"Not like she is now, mind you. But she was always tall, even though she didn't get any more food than the rest of us. Must be in the genes."

I looked down in thought. If not her name, then what? She hated and killed gang members, but then why join them? Whatever her secret was, it seemed like it would lie in her past. "Well, what about that night she killed all of those people? Did anything else happen?"

Her eyes turned to the side. "Not really."

"Can you tell me exactly what happened anyway?"

She let out a heavy sigh, but she stopped her work, resting it on her lap. "I don't see what good it'll do, but I can. It was eight years ago. We were all working like normal when they busted in with her. She was holding the kid, and they were threatening us and telling us what all would happen if we tried to run away. They were getting mad because the kid kept crying, but it she was just a toddler so what else could you expect?

They started beating on her and we all ran to hide in the back because we didn't want to be next. I remember it was so noisy, and then deathly silent. We were too afraid to come out. Then she must have gotten the axe. The other people started screaming and shots were being fired … We waited a long time after it was quiet to come out. By the time we did, they were all hacked up and she and the kid were gone. For a long time, we thought she actually got away."

I reflected on her words, but I didn't find any secrets. She didn't seem to know anything. I ran a hand through my hair. I wasn't coming back with as much information as I'd hoped.

At least it was something.

"I'm going to tell the Melechtions where you guys are but … do you want me to help you out right now?" I offered.

The silence I received stunned me. People looked down and away from me everywhere I turned.

The woman spoke up for them in the softest tone I'd yet heard from her, "They don't want to get caught."

I closed my eyes and took a deep breath. I was right there and knew they needed help, but I was powerless to protect them.

"Just hang in --"

As I started responding the front door clanked. She motioned for me to move and I ducked under her table. She threw a cloth over me and shoved me onto her pile of material. Two sets of footsteps entered the warehouse and paced the room.

"Hurry and eat, then get back to work." I recognized the gruff voice that gave them the warning, "You all know what happens if you don't."

Axe stalked through the room, tossing down packaged meals with Iona following her. She started on the other side of the room then came back around to our side. I crouched down, making myself as flat and blanket-like as possible. A box plopped on the table above me.

They didn't leave when the meals were distributed. She paced in the middle of the room while Iona leaned on the wall next to the entrance. Arms folded and face pinched, Axe walked too briskly to be relaxed.

Everyone kept to themselves, eating in silence. I played dead. Suddenly, she stomped towards our side of the building. I tensed as she walked by again.

She punched one of the crates. The woman at my table flinched. The crate creaked and toppled over. After that they collected the boxes and made a bee-line for the door.

No way was I going to hang out here. As soon as they closed the door I threw the cloth off and scrambled to the back. I climbed up the rickety platform I had created and hopped back out. I didn't worry about removing the clutter; I'd leave it there in case any of them decided to try and get out.

I stayed close to the wall, crouching by the front of the building to check if it was clear. A truck was still there, back facing the warehouse. Axe tossed a bunch of the boxes in the back.

"Hey, what's eating you?" Iona asked.

Axe threw another bundle of boxes in, shooting a glare in Iona's direction as she worked silently before turning away and folding her arms. "Have you ever thought of leaving?"

"You mean switching sides?" Iona put her hands on her hips. "I told you, Signe is the Scraper, she's the one who should be running things."

"Not that," Axe replied. "I don't care about any of that." She ground into the dirt with her foot. "I mean leave."

Iona tilted her head. "Why? Something wrong?"

She reached back, getting a grip on the axe and holding it out. She took some small swings with it. "It used to feel different. I used to feel good when I took out someone." She swung it down, chopping into the ground. "Now ... I can only feel mildly irritated that they're in the way."

Iona's response was delayed and cautious. "Something happen?"

Shaking her head as if to get rid of a bug, Axe glared at the ground. The handle of the axe slid through her fingers as she drew it back up. Her eyes fixed on it while she lifted it in front of her face.

"I don't know," she answered, gritting her teeth and growling the next part, "Something's wrong." She wrinkled her nose at axe.

Iona watched in silence, one hand holding her elbow and the other pressed against her cheek. While Axe turned the weapon in her hand with her eyes trained on the blade, Iona dropped her hands and walked towards her. Her expression of deep reflection melted into a smile. In a second her demeanor changed. The thoughtful, cautious person vanished, and the whimsical woman from before reappeared.

"You're probably just feeling burnt out," she assured her. She walked a few feet ahead of Axe and paused. Axe's eyes turned up from the blade. Iona shrugged and smiled coyly. "Anyway, we need to hurry up and deal with Lieran's people."

Her fingers played on the handle while she stared at Iona. A slight flush crept to her face while their eyes locked. Finally, she swung the Axe around and sheathed it, nodding.

I watched them get into the truck and drive away before making my way back to the city. Thoughts swirled through my head. I felt like I was lost at sea. Every time I tried to concentrate on one thought, others flooded in. The hostages, the kids, Valli, General Glaive ... In the span of days I'd witnessed and heard so many terrible things and I had no idea what to do. I was overwhelmed. I squeezed my hands together and wished for the Melechtions to run in and fix everything.

And Kelsy. I couldn't leave Kelsy there anymore

than any of the other people.

I went back to town and scribbled down as much information I could think of on a piece of paper – I even drew a map of the area. Once it was all down I headed to the hospital. The thought of running into Tyrus again made my skin tingle. *I hope one of the other ones is there.*

I got to the hospital, but my luck ran out when one of the nurses stopped me.

"Excuse me, where are you going?" he asked.

I had no excuse. Without Valli in the hospital I had no reason to be there.

"Um, I just have something to give to the Melechtions. I understand if I can't go up, but could you at least pass this on to them?" I held the piece of paper out for him but he didn't take it, looking puzzled.

"The Melechtions aren't here."

My eyes widened. "None of them?"

"No."

Why wouldn't any of them be here with General Glaive? Where are they?

"Well, can you give it to them when they come back?"

"I'm not sure if they will be back."

My ears slowly perked up. That was even stranger than them not being here to begin with.

"Is … General Glaive okay?" I couldn't think of what else to ask.

"I'm not at liberty to discuss that." He placed a

hand on my shoulder and began leading me out. "If that is all, then please head home. We're very busy."

With no other reason to stay, I did as he said and walked towards the hotel, mind boggled. It was hard to believe General Glaive would be left alone in the hospital without any guards. Could he have been transferred? Where were they all?

One last question pierced my mind. *Did they give up?*

With some food I picked up on the way, I went back to my room. Both of the kids were in front of the v-phone. The older was using the chair with the younger leaning on it next to him. My dad was on the video but he wasn't alone. He was accompanied by a familiar face, an old comrade of my dad's who moved when I was around eight, and was now in the same camp as him again.

"... Using her wit, she pretended that she couldn't see it. She told the doppelganger, 'Where? I don't see it.' The doppelganger tried to urge her to go in ..." my dad said, when his friend pitched in.

"It's right there in front of you, dear, just take a look," he used a higher-pitched voice with a shakiness to it.

"But she insisted that she couldn't see it. Finally, without thinking, the doppelganger moved forward to show her and fell into its own trap," Dad continued.

I recognized the story as one of the Twee Sister, a young girl who would outsmart various monsters. The two boys were enthralled as they listened, giving my dad and his friend their full attention. Listening to them calmed my nerves. I stayed quiet and set the food down in the kitchen as they told the end of the story.

When they finished I came over to the v-phone, standing by the chair and leaning down. "Thanks, Dad. I wasn't able to get anyone here yet, but I've got them for tonight."

I waved at his friend, who gave me a smile in return.

"Are you sure you have everything handled?" he asked.

"Yeah, I'll be fine." I turned to the kids. "There's some food on the table if you're hungry."

No sooner had I finished the sentence than they were off, and I took a seat in the chair. Dad's friend had also gotten up, leaving us somewhat alone.

"I tried to talk to the Melechtions but they weren't at the hospital anymore. I wonder if they moved the general," I told him.

"I still haven't heard anything about that. Are you sure you heard right?"

I was dumbstruck. Surely they should have heard by now. Something was really wrong with the whole picture.

"… Maybe. Something does seem really weird about it, but I don't know what exactly is going on." I slumped back in the chair, folding my arms and tilting my head back. "Either way, I'm exhausted. I can't wait to get to bed."

"Then I won't keep you. Take care of yourself, Leander."

"I will."

"I love you."

My eyes darted over to the kids who weren't paying attention anymore. "I love you, too."

The call was over. I stayed in place, worries nagging at my mind, before making a call.

It took a little bit for Ellora to pick up, but she looked curious rather than angry. "What are you calling about?"

"I have a question." I leaned forward. "Have you heard anything about General Glaive?"

Her eyes turned down and she shook her head as she answered, "What about him?"

"Anything about him getting hurt or something?"

"No, nothing like that. Why?"

Definitely strange. The news hadn't reached Dad's camp or the capital. Yet I saw it on the v-phone, and Tyrus had said it himself.

"Nevermind. Things have just been weird over here."

"How has Valli been doing?"

Her question startled me.

"He … hasn't been doing very well."

"Last I heard he was getting his operation. Did something go wrong?"

"Yeah, but, I'm trying to help out."

"Don't forget, if you let anything happen to him I'll have your head."

Ellora had been defensive of Valli before. I

nodded a little, and reached towards the v-phone. "I need to get going."

"All right then."

With our conversation over, I pondered what could be going on. Whatever it was, I wasn't going to figure it out sitting in a hotel room. I shuffled the kids off into a bath and took the time to relax and clear my mind. While I sat on the edge of the tub, I listened to the two bicker about the rules of a game they were making up. Eventually the older one won out and decided how the game would go and they settled down.

I closed my eyes and remembered bathing with my dad when I was younger. I often dictated what we would do in the bath, and decided who got what toys. He'd remark on my choices. Things like, "So I get the broken one?"

I was young, and I wasn't about to give him the best toys. Looking back on it now, it was more likely he was vaguely amused than upset; he probably found playing with toys in the tub boring.

The memories soothed my aching soul. My worries kept trying to peck their way back in. I'd take a deep breath and clear my thoughts only to have a thought of Valli, or the hostages, or General Glaive pop up.

Before I knew it, I was getting them out of the tub, rinsing them off, and wrapping towels around them. I got a shirt for each to wear to bed – since they were both quite small, my shirts covered them well enough. I took a short bath and headed to bed.

I heard them whispering in the bed next to mine. An occasional giggle rang out.

Despite all my fears, I fell asleep quickly.

12

The next morning I spent a long time staring at the ceiling. In a way, I just wanted to forget everything and go home, but the situation was too dire for me to give up. Lives hung in the balance and I needed to do what I could to help.

I gathered my thoughts. I needed to pass the information I had over to the Melechtions. What if they weren't here anymore? If they weren't at the hospital and the nurse wasn't sure if they'd be back, maybe General Glaive had been moved. Would they go with him or would they stay here and finish up the job?

I dug my fingers into the bed sheets. *Please let them still be here. I can't do this on my own.*

Finally I found the nerve to get up. I called Dad to let him know I was going out again. The scrap of paper in my pocket danced through my fingers. If they were still here, they'd be doing something at the warehouses, not loitering about town. I needed to scout around until I found them and avoid getting into trouble in the meantime.

I ate on the way. My mouth felt dry as I tried to swallow the sweet bread. I still didn't feel great after the fire from the other day. I downed a bottle of juice in one swig and let out a gasp. *I'll have to go easy on myself. I'm still hurt.* The thought made the whole situation worse. I didn't want to imagine running away again if I couldn't get enough air, and I had no reason to believe I wouldn't be killed.

I formed a map in my head of where to go first. I hopped on a cart and began my hunt.

After spending an hour perusing the outskirts of the city, I spotted something at one of the warehouses. A soldier had caught up with a fleeing suspect and tackled him at the door, pulling him back in.

They're here! The thought rang through my mind. *Some sort of scuffle?* I didn't know whether to flee or help. Neither seemed right. I didn't want to abandon them if they ran into trouble, but I wasn't a trained soldier, either. I decided to keep an eye on the situation to see if I could do anything.

I found myself pushing scraps around to climb in through a window, yet again. The warehouses were all similar in that way. Familiar crates were stacked to the side. I slid inside and dropped behind them.

I heard a commotion in the front. I paused, curiosity taking a firm hold with a strong urge to see what it was. I peeked through the door. The soldiers were doing the ambushing. Fast, not giving them a chance to counterattack, they had several down and were securing them. While they secured those another was fighting. His leg was sliced, and in the fray, he limped towards the back room.

"Tyrus," was the only word I discerned before I ran back and dove behind some crates. I didn't want to get caught in the middle of a fight.

The man stumbled into the room, faltering because of his injured leg. Not far behind, Tyrus rushed in with his gun out. After watching the man for a few moments, he put the gun away and reached for his knife. He prowled, eying the man up and down while the man tried to get away. Tyrus waited a long time. For a while, I wondered if he was afraid to get into a fight, but that changed in a flash.

Just as the man attempted to climb for the window Tyrus bolted in, slicing his side and throwing him to the ground. He didn't go for another stab, though. He backed up and watched the man attempt to get back up. I started to feel sorry for the man, struggling desperately in a hopeless situation. I remained calm by telling myself he was likely a cold-blooded murderer.

Tyrus toyed with him, letting him flail about only to cut him down again.

Dorrius appeared in the doorway. From there, he watched Tyrus play his game. He let it go on for a minute before calling out, "Tyrus! That's enough. We need to finish up here."

Tyrus finally noticed the extra presence, pausing to put the knife away and get some cuffs out. Dorrius joined him, taking the man by the arm to drag him back to the other room, but Tyrus stayed behind, fidgeting.

The second Dorrius reached the door, Tyrus began heading towards the back of the room, where the man had tried to escape through the window. He moved too soon, though. Dorrius's ear flicked and he glanced back. He called Quinn over, handing over the man before turning back.

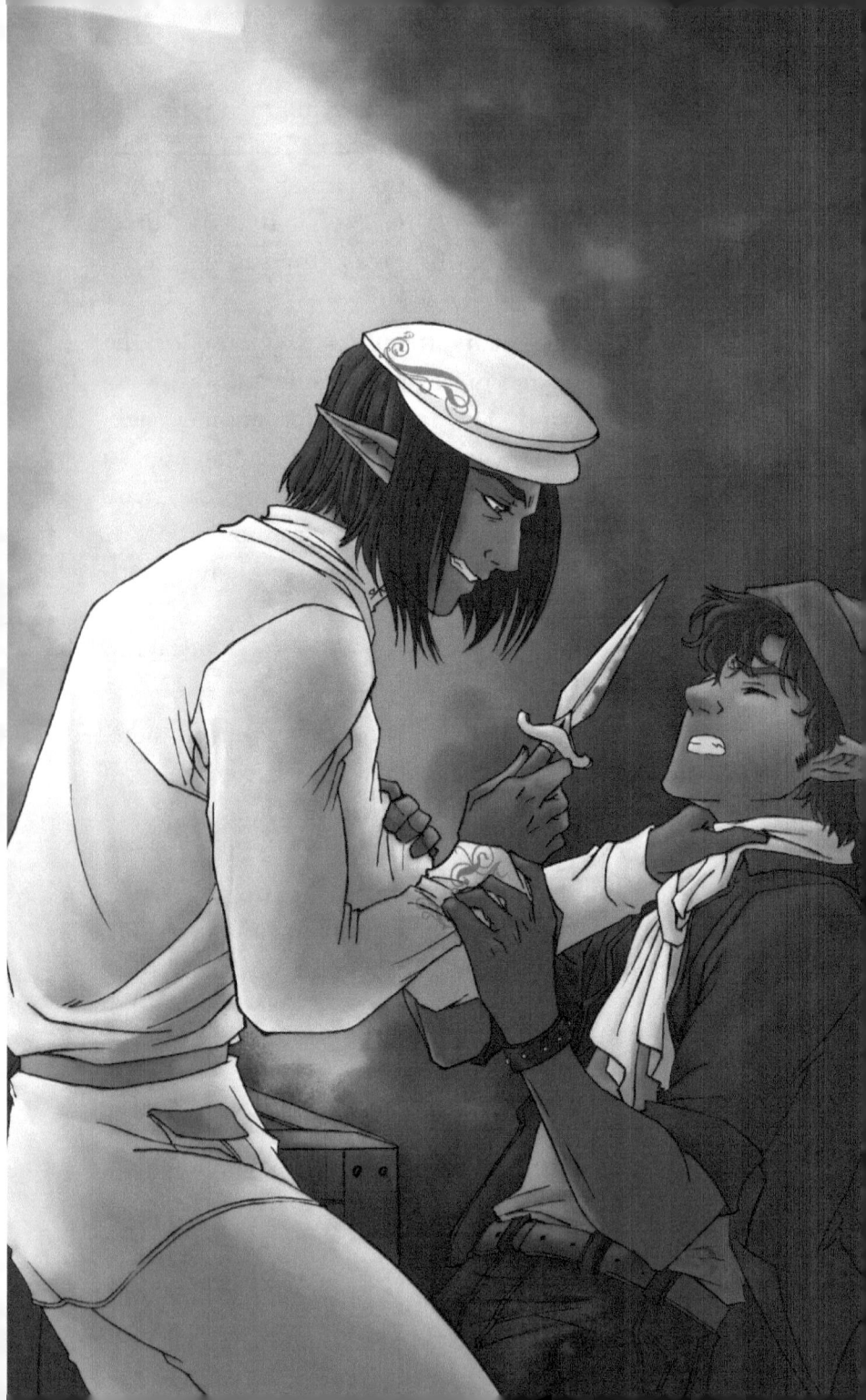

"Tyrus, what's going on?" He stepped back into the room.

Stopping to turn around, Tyrus looked flustered. "I have to get out of here."

"Why?" He took a few slow strides towards Tyrus, keeping a large distance.

"There's been a mistake. I don't belong here! What is General Glaive going to do to me when he figures it out?" he lashed out, voice loud and quaking.

Dorrius knit his brows. "He's already picked you. You're part of the group."

"I can't keep up, though. He's going to change his mind." He paced hastily on the other side of the room. "What's he going to do then? I could end up like all those soldiers who disappear."

Dorrius stood in place, eyes following Tyrus as he spoke in a calm voice, "You'll be fine. General Glaive doesn't do that."

"What about the soldiers who go missing?" His movements were shaking and spastic, like he was trapped and waiting for an escape.

"It's not like that. Those are just rumors," Dorrius assured him. "The soldiers who 'disappear' simply moved away."

"They'd leave their jobs because of that?" he challenged.

"I'm sure you could understand. You've been through his interview."

There was an awkward silence as Tyrus tilted his head, pressing his lips together, eyes roaming. He paused his pacing. "But I already messed up. At the town hall. I didn't find that guy. You and Quinn got him."

"Quinn and I have been working together long before General Glaive became the general. We've spent the last couple of years with each other every day. We knew each other inside and out. All it took was a glance for him to know I wanted the rest of you to keep walking. You've only been with us a couple weeks. In time you'll learn, just like Giddeon did." Dorrius gave a soft smile, taking a step closer.

"Giddeon is smarter than me. He's stronger. He's taller. I don't measure up," he objected.

"Do you know what General Glaive wants more than any of that?" Dorrius continued to walk, slowly decreasing the space between them.

Tyrus raised an eyebrow.

"He wants loyalty. People he can trust. It doesn't matter if you have the smartest man in the universe if he'll turn on you. That's what he tests in his interview. Listen and do your best and you should be fine."

"But what if I can't do something?" he strangled out the question.

"He's not as bad as you think he is. He doesn't dole out punishments for no reason. He's reasonable in what he expects from us," Dorrius explained.

Tyrus hesitated.

"Don't throw away the opportunity of a lifetime on an impulse." Dorrius extended an arm, inviting Tyrus to join him.

"You're going to tell the general." Tyrus arched a brow, staying away.

"I won't tell the general."

Eye narrowed, Tyrus scrutinized him.

"I don't need to. The general expects us to be able to handle ourselves," Dorrius reassured him. After a brief pause, Tyrus stepped forward. Dorrius swept around him, following him as they headed towards the door. They were at the threshold when I poked my head high enough above the boxes for my eyes to show.

"Dorrius?" my voice barely squeaked out, but I spoke a moment too soon. I caught Tyrus's attention as well. When both turned my way, I ducked back down.

The footsteps approached and hiding seemed useless. I peeked above the box.

Tyrus' mood swung again as he looked down at me then up at Dorrius quizzically. "Can we arrest him this time?"

"Hold off," Dorrius answered holding up a hand towards him and looking to me. "Explain yourself."

"I have information." I held up my scrap of paper, safely behind my wooden fortress.

Dorrius nodded towards Tyrus. "Go help the others. I'll handle this."

To my relief, Tyrus walked towards the door with one glance back before leaving. With a hand on the box I pushed myself up, looking up at Dorrius. I felt even smaller than usual as I leaned forward to hand him the scrap. He accepted it, glancing down with his head still held high.

"I-it has a list of all the places I think they're holding people." I failed to keep my voice steady. I had no idea if, yet again, the information I was providing them was something they already knew.

He gave me a nod as he read, then put the note in his pocket. "It's dangerous here. I don't think you quite understand how violent these people are. Go back to your hotel and stay safe."

When he turned to leave I spoke up, making my own heart jump, "D-Dorrius?"

He glanced over his shoulder and I shrank away.

"If General Glaive isn't so bad, why doesn't he squash the rumors about him?"

He paused, holding his arms behind his back. "You're familiar with Wilten Crags?"

The image of the desecrated city popped in my head, causing me to inwardly flinch. I nodded at him. I knew it all too well.

"Do you understand why that happened?"

I furrowed my brows. "Wasn't it corrupt scientists?"

"It was the beginning of King Lariat's reign. He hadn't even lived in the castle before that. He came in with high hopes and tried to encourage scientists to find cures by offering a reward. Invigorated, scientists everywhere began working. Wilten Crags was one of those places. They were trying to find a cure for a lung disease and were working with a few patients.

Some of those patients passed and they didn't have enough test subjects. Without more subjects they couldn't get the data they needed for the reward, so they created more subjects. It was just the first in a line of terrible things they did. General Glaive believes they saw King Lariat's kindness for weakness.

They weren't afraid of him, so they thought they could do whatever they wanted and people died. Criminals need to fear retribution. The general has no time to appear soft. He believes it's better for people to fear him." He lifted his chin.

"Do you believe that?"

"I have my own opinions, but I follow the general."

"So the rumors about him aren't true?"

"Some are; some aren't."

"Is he ... okay?" I moved an inch forward.

"We can't discuss that."

"Tyrus said he was shot in the head ... but he was smiling when he said it."

Dorrius pursed his lips, looking troubled.

"Don't concern yourself with that. Get out of here."

He gestured and I followed his arm, looking back up at the window.

I'd done what I could for the hostages. That left Kelsy. Unlike the others she was mixed up with the gang members. I didn't want to see her caught in the middle of a fight.

Being able to climb out the window without hiding was a welcome relief. I hopped out, stood in a place for a moment to recover, and began my walk back to Kelsy.

13

Just one more thing, then you can take a break. I still hadn't found Valli or any hints about Valli, but I didn't know what to do about it. I could at least get Kelsy to safety, though.

I showed up at the empty warehouse and went in. I was about to climb into the vent when I heard steps behind me. Before I had a chance to react, something heavy and hard slammed into the wall next to me.

I jumped to the side, stumbling down the crates I had been on. It wasn't as empty as I'd thought.

Back against the wall, I looked straight at Axe and Iona. Signe and the other driver came around from the back. I'd been too careless. My eyes darted to the exit. I couldn't see any way to get to it safely. Without thinking, I pounded on the wall under the vent, hoping to attract Kelsy's attention.

"What's going on here?" Signe asked.

"This guy is sneaking into our place," Axe said as she approached. Iona used the back of a truck as a seat while she cleaned a pistol. I banged on the wall again.

"Hey, what do you think you're doing?"

"Nothing. Nothing at all!" My voice trembled.

Kelsy poked her head out of the vent before hopping down. Axe immediately lowered her arm half way.

"What's going on?" Kelsy asked.

"Just dealing with a break-in," Axe answered.

She glanced up at me before looking back at them. "He's not breaking in. He's my friend." She jumped off the box to the ground.

"Your friend?" Axe cocked an eyebrow.

"Yeah, we've been talking," she replied cheerfully.

The man stepped towards her with his fists clenched. "You stupid kid, you gave away our information!" Kelsy backed away with a small cry, until an axe slammed down between them. They both jumped. Axe lowered her head to glare at him eye to eye.

"You can't defend her forever," he spat before skulking off. She relaxed as he walked away.

Axe peered down at Kelsy from the corner of her eye. "You need to get stronger."

"We can't have her running around telling everyone our business!" He flung his arm out towards Kelsy, complaining to Signe.

She smacked him across the back of the head. "Learn your place. You're only a driver. You have no place to complain."

He looked confused momentarily, glancing at Iona. "But she's a driver and she complains."

"She also gathers information and found the necklace." Signe pointed directly in his face. "All you do is drive. You're *replaceable*."

He backed away and quieted.

"Iona, why don't you take Kelsy out?" Axe recommended.

I realized the only thing keeping me alive was the fact that Kelsy was still in the room. I hated to use an eight-year-old but I had to keep her there for my own safety.

Just as Iona was setting down the gun with a few others, I shouted, "Wait!"

It gave them a momentary pause. I needed to think of something to keep them there. "Why don't we work on that outfit?" I offered Kelsy.

"Go outside and play, Kelsy. We have to talk business here," Axe told her.

She looked between us but turned to go out with Iona again. I stared after her. I needed something more, anything that would work. I looked at the short little girl, and then back at the woman in front of me, itching to pull the axe off her back. Suddenly, something struck me.

"Wait!" I shouted again and Kelsy glanced back. With her round face and nose that turned up slightly at the end. I glanced back at Axe, with her long nose and oval face, narrowing my eyes slightly. I knew something was wrong, and I finally figured out what it was.

"Your sister is dead," I told Axe pointedly. The years had been wrong. If her sister was a toddler when she tried to escape eight years ago, Kelsy shouldn't have just turned eight. And there was no reason a baby would stop crying in the middle of a fight. And she and

Kelsy looked nothing alike.

Kelsy looked confused when she responded, "No I'm not. I'm right here."

Axe lunged at me, pressing the axe forward so the curve between the blades was pressed against my neck. She shot a glare towards Signe, who shrugged in response. "Don't look at me, I never said anything."

"What's going on?" Kelsy started walking back, puzzled. I winced. I didn't want to hurt her.

"Don't worry about it, Kelsy," Axe growled.

A rumbling outside reached our ears. Vehicle engines came close then flicked off. The others exchanged glances before Signe ordered the man, "See who it is."

The man climbed up to the window, but what he answered wasn't what any of us were expecting. "It's the general and his soldiers!"

Suddenly I was an afterthought.

"You're sure?" Signe questioned.

"Yes, they just pulled up in some trucks and vans," he answered. A momentary silence covered the room.

"Get out, I'll hold them off," Axe ordered. She moved to the back of the truck, where Iona held up a gun for her. Their hands touched briefly when she took the gun and seemed to linger longer than needed. Iona tried to keep a confident look but stress lines gave her away. Their eyes met, and Axe smiled softly as she pulled the gun away. I wasted no time finding some cover while they were distracted.

Iona hopped off the back of the truck and the group began heading for the back before Axe interrupted them, "There's probably some behind the building. Use the tunnel."

"Tunnel?" Iona asked. The man seemed confused as well, but Signe waved them over to the vent.

"Hurry it up," she demanded. "We'll head to the factory and gather *everyone*."

As the others crawled out, Axe grabbed her helmet and went to the entrance with weapon loaded. She seemed fearless in her armor.

I climbed to the rafters while I had the chance. I wasn't sure what to do. We were probably surrounded and the only escape was full of dangerous people. I found a spot where I could see out the window.

Axe burst through the doors and ducked behind sparse cover quickly. The soldiers had three vehicles: two trucks, and one for emergency supplies. Each had a door open and they were using them as shields. It looked as if there was a soldier behind each door except for one which had two.

She raised the pistol and aimed at one of the doors. The soldiers stayed in their positions. She pulled the trigger and I covered my ears to protect them from the thunderous sound.

A sound that never came. It looked like she pulled it but nothing happened. She shook the gun and smacked the hilt with the palm of her hand.

She threw it to the ground and knelt in a stunned silence for a moment. General Glaive took a few steps out from behind his door, proving once again he was capable of smiling with the slightest, barely discernible curve of his lips. The other three stepped out, staying by their vehicles.

At first, she took one step back, reaching for the axe at the same time. A realization seemed to dawn on her when she whipped her head around to face the open door.

"Kelsy!" she yelled. Her effort was fruitless – the others had already gone.

She drew the axe and got into a fighting stance. I knew well from before she wouldn't back down just because they had guns. General Glaive didn't draw a weapon.

When she left her cover to go after him he raised his right hand.

In an instant she hit the ground. I didn't understand why at first. She was charging and then she collapsed but none of them had fired.

Her hand went to her side, grabbing it and pulling away as she writhed on the ground. It was then I could see the blood. Something had hit her in the side. I looked over the soldiers but not all of them were there.

The wound didn't stop her. She forced herself to her feet and fled back into the warehouse. As soon as she entered, I pulled away from the window to hide. She ran behind a bunch of the boxes. Soldiers entered the room carrying rifles. They paused to kneel, aim, and check the area.

"Stay alert. Time is on our side," Glaive told his

men as they began making their way around the room with slow, cautious steps, guns raised. Each went a different direction.

Quinn broke further from the group as he headed towards the back. I would have thought nothing of it if it weren't for what happened next. With a crash, a barrel of oil slammed into the ground next to him. The top popped off and liquid splashed all over him as he stepped back and held up an arm to cover his face. He glanced down at himself, seeming more curious about the liquid than anything else.

That split second seemed to drag on forever. Axe flicked a match over the boxes. Everyone realized what was about to happen. Before the flame hit General Glaive shouted, "Cover me!" and he sprinted across the room towards Quinn.

In the second the flame took to hit the oil, Quinn attempted to run away, yanking off his dampened jacket as he did. The jacket flew behind him when he tossed it aside. When the oil burst into flames the garment was quickly caught in the fire. He couldn't run fast enough. The flames swarmed him and he dove to the ground away from the puddle of oil, rolling around while he screamed.

Dorrius kept his gun trained on the area while Tetchion searched for something to put out the fire with. General Glaive reached him in little time, tearing off his own jacket and placing it over the man. He smothered the flames, pulling Quinn farther away from the fire. The top of his body was mostly untouched, but the lower half had been consumed for a short time. His pants were burned and wrecked.

Glaive pulled out his dagger and sliced the pants off.

"Can you feel this?" he asked.

"Yes!" the man cried loudly.

"Good, then your nerve endings are still there."

"I wish they weren't!" Quinn spat back as he lay back and moaned in pain. His hands clenched at his head.

General Glaive forgave the outburst, ordering the other soldiers, "Take care of him."

Dorrius ran over while Tetchion brought an extinguisher and began attacking the fire. They maintained composure, even though their movements were hurried.

The general put his rifle away and drew his sword along with a dagger. He ran towards the back.

"Quick, get some small boxes," Dorrius said as he examined Quinn. They found different items and placed them around, lifting up Quinn's limbs even as he whimpered.

"Second and first degree. We have some water in the ambulance. We need to transport him to the hospital immediately. Hurry and get the stretcher."

Tetchion ran out to the vehicles, leaving Quinn with Dorrius.

On the other side of the warehouse, General Glaive raced towards the back exit. He bounded over a set of boxes and cut off Axe. She stopped and they glared at each other. Her figure was slumped, her axe nearly dragging on the floor.

Glaive raised his weapons silently, and though I couldn't see his expression I felt and air of anger from him.

Axe straightened up and pulled her hand away from her side with great effort. She plastered a layer of blood on the handle of her axe when she grabbed it with her second hand. She might have been an inch or two taller than Glaive at full height, but she didn't make him look small by any means.

She took the first strike, swinging low. He backed out of reach in one quick, trained move. The next swing came from above and he deflected it with his dagger, lunging forward and thrusting with the sword.

Slow and shaky, she didn't dodge the stab to her abdomen. The sword plunged straight through her armor.

She drew back, keeling over more with the axe still weakly gripped in one hand. She attempted another swing but it was no use. Glaive knocked it away and stabbed her in the side before kicking her down. His motions were so precise, and hers so chaotic.

Bleeding profusely, she strove to get back up to no avail. General Glaive glared down at her coldly.

With her taken care of, General Glaive threw open the back door and called out, "Giddeon, get in here. Quickly!"

Giddeon rushed in from the back. "No one came this way."

General Glaive brushed away the momentary

confusion. "There must have been another exit. Quinn was injured. Help carry him out. We'll regroup after we get him to the hospital."

Tetchion rolled in a stretcher, and they carefully lifted Quinn onto it. As Tetchion and Giddeon began pushing him out, Tyrus entered from the front, rifle in hand. He walked briskly onto the scene. Dorrius met him halfway.

"That was a good shot." Dorrius reached out to touch his shoulder. Tyrus glanced at the hand as Dorrius continued, "It gets easier over time."

"What does?" Tyrus sounded confused.

"Shooting people."

"Oh," he answered flatly. "It wasn't that hard of a shot."

Tyrus continued past him towards the others. Dorrius' eyes lingered on him, expression stern before following.

"What happened here?" Tyrus asked curiously while he watched them move Quinn.

"Quinn was burned."

"Oh." Tyrus tilted his head, looking more intrigued than concerned. "No one ever came out the back."

"They probably had another exit. We'll figure out what to do about them after we deal with Quinn," Glaive explained.

"What about the one I shot?"

"If she survives we'll save her for the Hold," Glaive told him. "We're heading out."

The soldiers began trickling out, but Dorrius lagged behind. General Glaive noticed and stopped, looking to him.

When they were alone – or so they believed – Dorrius approached him.

"General," he said simply.

"Hmm?"

"I'm concerned about Tyrus."

"What about him?"

"He seems to lack empathy."

Glaive eyes focused on his man and he nodded his head gently when he responded, "I thought as much."

"What should we do?" Dorrius asked.

"He's one of you. Make him a part of your group," the general answered bluntly.

"But how can I do that if he doesn't feel anything for anyone?"

"He feels for himself. He'll have everything he's ever wanted as long as he follows orders. Make sure he remembers that, and make sure he realizes he'll lose it all if he doesn't," Glaive answered, meeting his eyes. "Just don't expect him to ever care about you."

Dorrius folded his arms, eyes scouring the ground for answers. "This will be challenging. No one has ever attempted something like this before."

"You're the psychologist. You figure it out," the general quipped.

"May I ask why him?"

"… He's different. His mind works in a way that

normal people wouldn't expect. We'll have an opportunity to understand him better, but our enemies won't. They won't be able to predict the way he thinks. It might save us one day." He glanced back. "It doesn't hurt that he's a talented sniper."

"Hmm," Dorrius continued to mull it over.

"We don't have time right now. We need to take Quinn." The general cut the conversation short.

"We still haven't determined what killed Lieran, either," Dorrius agreed as they moved out.

Their conversation faded as they headed out.

In their absence, I dropped from the rafters. The place was a mess, burned and stained. Suddenly, I had one rare opportunity to ask Axe some questions, if she was alive.

I knelt by her body. She seemed to be unconscious, lying face down. Blood was all over. Her helmet had rolled off of her head.

Opening a crate, I ripped off pieces of cloth and tried to bandage her, then ran over to the sink and poured some water into one of their dishes.

I tugged her over and put the bowl to her lips. Some consciousness seemed to come back to her. Her eyes didn't open but her mouth reacted, taking in a little bit of the water as more dribbled down her front and over the armor.

I went back to applying pressure to the wound on her side. Her eyes blinked then opened half way. This was my chance. My one chance to finally ask her about Valli.

"Where's Valli?" I snapped at her.

A crinkle formed on her forehead as she looked around. Her hand moved to her stomach. When she lifted it up it had blood on it. She held it up, looking at her palm, before using the same hand to push her hair back. She left a smear of blood across one side of her face and through her hair.

I ignored the blood, grabbing her shoulder and pulling her. She was heavy, not easy for someone small like me to yank around even if she was debilitated. "Where's Valli?"

Her eyes focused more on me, a mixture of irritation and confusion crossing her face. "Who?"

"Valli!" It came to mind that she wouldn't know his name. "He was with me before I hit you with the truck! Where is he?"

"How should I know? I haven't seen him since then," she snapped.

I froze in stunned silence. The entire time I'd operated on the assumption that she and her friends had gone back and found him, or at least knew what happened. Her words sent a whole new possibility piercing through me.

"You're lying!" I shouted.

"Heh." She laid her head back on the floor, staring straight up. "Think what you want."

With my hand pressed against her side, my mind went through the possibilities. *Did he try to walk back on his own? Did he not make it?* I'd have to search the area between the warehouse and the town, making sure not to miss any spots. The amount of land worried me; I couldn't assume he went in a perfectly straight line. He could have gotten lost, or wandered slightly off the path. He could have fallen over anywhere.

An eerie silence covered the warehouse as horrible thoughts filled my mind and she stared up at the ceiling.

She was the one who broke the silence with a quiet, pensive, "I never felt anything for her."

It broke me out of my thoughts. *Kelsy?*

After a few more breaths she continued, "She was never what she was meant to be."

I narrowed my eyes and held my tongue. *Of course, you can't just replace one kid with another.*

"I never meant for things to go this way." As she began pushing herself up into a sitting position I backed away. "All I ever wanted was to get Kelsy and be left alone. To fix things." She let out a snort full of contempt. "Not that any of them understood that. Why would they care, anyway? Greedy little snipes, they'll do anything to get what they want." As the anger grew in her voice I backed farther away. She wrestled with her broken body, fumbling to her feet despite all logic dictating that it would be a bad idea. "Eight years. *Eight years* it's been nothing but an act. And for what?" She let out a huff, arm indicating the room around her. "For *this?*"

She bent over, grabbing the axe from the ground with one hand and the helmet with the other. I wanted to stop her, but I was afraid of a direct confrontation. Injured or not, she could still hurt me, but if I kept my distance I could outrun her.

She lifted the axe with the pommel resting on

the ground, eyes fixed on the blade where her reflection was. I stayed in a crouched position, ready to bolt at the first hint of danger.

The laughter that rang out from her sent a jolt through me. She threw her head back, unrestrained cackles filling the air. *She's gone mad!* I thought, *Assuming she wasn't already mad to begin with.*

When the laughter died down, she slipped the helmet over her blood encrusted hair, sneering at the reflection. "But I hacked down more of them than anyone. I was the top, the most feared, the stuff of nightmares." She paused her gloating, whispering in a wistful voice, "I haven't felt like this in a long time."

With her axe occasionally dragging on the ground, she began stumbling forward. For a second my thoughts turned from fear to wondering how far she could walk before she fell over.

I kept my distance, my curiosity besting me as she reached the door. "Where are you going?"

She glanced back, a wild smirk on her face. "I'm going to get the person who betrayed me."

Time slowed while I watched her stagger away, out of the building to some unknown destination. Who? I pondered before brushing the thought aside. It didn't matter. What mattered now was that Kelsy was still in danger, more danger than before. Whatever fight they were about to get into, I had to get her out of there.

14

Long before I arrived at the factory, I saw trucks and people going in the same direction. Instinct screamed at me to hide, but few people would recognize me. So I followed the crowd, intending to blend in. After several minutes I made my way over to a group.

"What's with all this?" I asked, trying to stay as vague as possible.

A woman in the group glanced over at me. "No idea. The Scraper is demanding everyone gather up. I'm just curious what's going on."

Another in the group piped up, "What's with the message about the general? I thought he was supposed to be dead."

"I don't know. Maybe we'll get an explanation when we get there."

I nodded despite not knowing what they meant.

Soon we merged with the stream of people flowing in from all directions. When we reached the factory, thousands of people were gathered around it and more kept coming.

I held my jacket around myself tightly. I didn't recognize them, but they also didn't recognize me. I was just another face in the crowd. More and more, I was immersed in a sea of gangsters. The woman next to me stopped and folded her arms, putting more weight on one leg as we waited.

Heads turned up and I followed suit. Signe stood on the roof with her leg up on the ledge, looking down at us. Iona, her driver, and Kelsy were behind her.

"Listen up," she called down to us all. The murmurs of the crowd died down. "Soon the general will be dead, and then we'll have no limitations. We will expand. We will grow. We won't run a small part of this country. We'll run the whole country. This city is just the start! And I know how to do it." She brought down her leg and strode to the side. "We'll start getting people in the army. We'll get real weapons that put these to shame." She held up a pistol, dangling it by two fingers as if it was diseased. "We'll have vehicles. Armor. Weapons. Ammunition. We will be unstoppable."

Cheers erupted from the crowd. Or, at least, some of them. The woman I had followed stared up with a sullen expression and her arms folded. Others scattered around responded with the same lack of enthusiasm.

"What's wrong?" I asked her.

"As if a seventeen-year-old knows how to do that," she muttered. "Lieran should be running this."

A man bumped my shoulder as people shuffled to the side. Moving with them, I searched for the reason everyone was stepping aside. In the middle of the crowd, Darora Seer walked through the path they'd made to the entrance. His eyes darted all over as he passed. Signe and the others disappeared from the roof.

"What's Darora Seer doing here?" I whispered.

The woman shrugged. "The Scraper must need to talk to him." I looked around at the crowd. No one else seemed surprised by his appearance.

I began making my way through the crowd towards the entrance. I'd barely gone a few feet when phones were ringing everywhere.

Not everyone's, though. I stopped to see if I could catch a glimpse of the message they received. I couldn't get a good view, but I saw the response.

The woman I followed put her phone away and turned to leave.

"Where do you think you're going?" Another woman stepped in front of her.

"Lieran has called for a meeting." She glared down her nose at her.

"Lieran is dead!" the other snapped back.

"The general was supposedly dead, too."

Lieran is dead. General Glaive's men wouldn't lie to him about it. But then … The message must be sent by them.

For some reason the general wanted them to believe Lieran was still alive, so with my chest tightening up on me, I piped up and lied, "I saw him heading south just a little bit ago."

The lie confirmed their doubts about his death. All around the group began to pull apart at the seams, with hundreds of people making moves to leave.

"We have orders to deal with anyone who goes against Signe," the woman warned her, putting a finger in her face.

She quirked a brow, lifting her chin and daring

her, "Try me."

A punch flew. One, two, three … suddenly masses of people were jumping in on the brawl. I covered my head and wove through the crowd towards the door.

A wisp of air grazed my back as a punch whooshed above me. I fell to my knees and crawled until I reached an opening. Just as I began getting up, a person tripped over me, shoving me back to the ground. He scrambled to his feet and disappeared in the frenzy while I lay on my side. With a grunt I pushed myself back up.

Through the crowd, I caught a glimpse of the familiar white and red. A tall man, being ignored in the chaos of the infighting, was working his way through. As far as I could see neither his gun nor sword were on him.

The general. He was moving in the same direction I was now, and Darora Seer had earlier. Seeing him heading through the fray, seemingly unarmed and alone, left me stunned for a moment, but my mind fled back to Kelsy. I slipped through the entrance.

Almost everyone was outside fighting, so I found myself standing at the entrance, alone. The doors closed behind me with a thud. Signe's voice echoed faintly through the factory.

I poked my head out from behind a machine to see Signe on the catwalk racing to the ground floor with the other three following her. Darora Seer stood in the middle of the factory, watching them.

"Where's Sissy?" Kelsy asked while trotting on their heels. Her question was ignored.

"How come Sissy isn't here yet?" Kelsy tried again.

Signe shot a sharp glare in her direction and gave a pointed response, "I'll let you know if I'm interested in talking to you."

Kelsy quieted, head down. I gritted my teeth. What value did she have to them without Axe? I could see her future spiraling downward very quickly.

I crept upstairs while they went down, looking for some way to get Kelsy out of there. And Darora … I considered it. He was in danger as well, but he was also a participant.

No. I'm not going to be the one who makes that judgment. I'll get them both out. I swallowed my distaste for the noble and carried on.

I looked for some way I could bring them up to the walkway from below and noticed the controls to the cranes on the ceiling, but I doubted they had any power. I touched the control box, wondering if I could find some way to use them.

"Darora Seer," Signe spoke in a loud voice that filled the factory. "You have one simple job. Keep the government out of our business." The moment her foot touched the ground, she flew towards him at a speed that made him step backwards. "If you can't even do that," she narrowed her eyes, "what do we need you for?"

He held up his hands as he backed away, putting a small amount of space between them. "There wasn't anything I could do. I've been *trying* …"

"The *general* has been poking around. It doesn't get any worse than that."

"Surely you can't expect me to give orders to the general. I can still try to convince him that he isn't needed here."

"Too late for that. I'll take care of him myself."

"What if he doesn't get the message?" Iona asked from behind her.

"I made sure it was spread around to everyone." Ahe frowned. "I have a feeling he'll get it."

"And if he doesn't?" Iona pressed further.

"That's too bad. I'll start killing people anyway." Her gaze turned back to Darora. "I can start with this one."

"Hold on!" Darora pleaded. "Even if you do kill the general, you're still going to need someone. Most of the nobles aren't fond of him anyway. I can smooth things over and make it sound like some sort of accident."

Then General Glaive made his entrance. When the doors opened the ruckus of outside grew louder momentarily. He approached with confidence, unarmed.

"General!" Darora yelped.

General Glaive remained silent, eyes moving to Darora. With a single arched eyebrow he said simply, "Darora Seer."

"It's not what it looks like." Darora was completely flustered. "You don't understand. It was just a small thing at first ... approving a person here, vouching for someone there. I had to do it to keep things going. And then it got out of control ..."

"I'll deal with you later," he replied with an edge of impatience. "I'm going to make an example out of you."

Darora Seer slunk back.

Signe laid her eyes on him, a smug grin crossing her face. "You're looking healthy for a man with a bullet in his head."

General Glaive stayed silent.

She pointed the gun towards the sky while she strutted. With General Glaive unarmed, he stood opposite Signe, Iona and the driver, all with guns. Behind them, Kelsy and Darora attempted to stay back, ready to take cover.

I grabbed hold of a lever and jiggled it, but nothing happened.

"Whoever's in control makes the rules." Signe wagged her gun. "And I'm in control."

General Glaive stood still, hands behind his back as his eyes followed her every stride.

"This is *my* territory." She threw her hands out. "You can't be that bright if you came here yourself. And what for? To try and save a couple of lives?" she mocked him, wrinkling her nose.

Silence. When she didn't get a response her expression fell. "What's wrong with you? Nothing to say for yourself?"

"I don't answer to children," he stated.

Her irritation quickly turned to anger. She swung her arm down and a shot rang out. He stepped to the side as she did, the bullet whizzing past him as he maintained composure.

She glared at him with the gun still held out. "This is war, and I don't have to follow the rules like you."

"You're assuming there are rules in war," he sullenly replied. "There aren't."

Iona moved near the tanks as they argued.

"That doesn't really matter. Because I'm going to be here, and you aren't," Signe told him. As she lowered the gun to shoot again Iona slammed down a lever. Tanks gurgled; lights flickered on; and the whirr of the conveyor belts filled the air. Signe's eyes darted everywhere as the factory roared to life.

Iona slid a handgun across the floor to General Glaive. He picked it up and the tides had changed. He was no longer outnumbered and out-armed.

Seeing the change, the driver bolted towards the entrance and Iona chased after him, leaving the general and the Scraper. Signe and General Glaive both dove for cover.

I yanked the lever to the side, moving one of the cranes above where Kelsy and Darora were and lowered it, running over to the side of the walkway to get their attention.

"Kelsy!" I yelled down at them, not worried about my voice carrying too far over all the mechanical sounds. Kelsy flicked an ear before looking up. Her movements caught Darora's attention, and he looked up, too.

"The crane!" I pointed at it, worried that she wouldn't hear me.

The hook hit the ground and the wires holding it began sagging like a limp noodle. They both grabbed wires. Darora placed his foot in the curve of the hook and Kelsy stepped on top of him. I hit the button to raise it.

While it was lifting them an explosion deafened us. One of the tanks, which seemed to be melting sand, groaned. For a brief moment, a sliver of red liquid glowed through a crack in the tank. It seeped out like a fire in gel form. Then a squeal that rivaled the explosion screeched through the building as the gigantic tank began tipping over. The lava-like substance oozed out onto the floor as the container split apart. The tank knocked over everything in its way. At the top, a pipe that reached the ceiling rammed through cables and rails while the rest of the tank dragged down walkways.

I half fell and half floundered to the side of the catwalk, reaching over the fence as the rail holding the crane was knocked off the ceiling. I grabbed Kelsy's arm and held onto her as the crane slid down the rail. Darora sailed a few feet before letting go of the crane and falling to the floor.

The walkway bounced under me, dislodged by the tank. It tilted and swayed. Once I got my balance back, I pushed against the fence and pulled Kelsy up. I grabbed the side and held onto Kelsy with all of my strength until it stopped swinging, glancing down at

Darora on the floor, yards away from where melted sand was pouring out and Signe and General Glaive were fighting.

He made this mess, he'll have to live with it, I told myself. With the vent covered in a boiling brew and more people beginning to spill into the building as they fought, I had no idea where to go to escape.

I held Kelsy's hand and began to guide her one way but she resisted.

"This way!" she said, pulling me along. I let her lead since she knew the place better than I did. The grating clanked as we ran towards the side of the room opposite the tank, fleeing from the steaming heat. The platform we were on had been pulled out of place and no longer connected on the other side like it was supposed to. Instead, the jagged end hung uselessly in the air.

Above us, another walkway was going the opposite way. It was the only way I could see to keep moving, but it was too high for me to reach.

"Here," I told Kelsy, kneeling down and holding out my hands to give her a boost up. She grabbed what was left of a support beam hanging from the above catwalk to steady herself until she could reach the platform. I hoisted her as much as possible until she got her arms over the edge and pulled herself up.

I looked for a way to get myself up, balancing on the swaying catwalk. For a moment I thought I was stuck, when a hook lowered from the ceiling. I glanced up, and Kelsy peeked over the fence at me. The hook

continued lowering. I grabbed it and pulled it towards me, setting it on the floor in front of me as the cord began going slack.

Kelsy disappeared again and the cable started pulling up. I set my foot in the hook and hung on, grabbing the walkway as soon as I was high enough and jumping when I had a good grip. I climbed over the fence and joined her.

We took the catwalk to the front part of the factory. The path had been rammed by another walkway, twisting it out of place. The end was displaced and no longer attached to the stairs. We ran to the edge and watched the chaos unfolding below. Signe bounded across a conveyor belt behind us. I didn't see the general.

Fingers wrapped around the railing, I tried to come up with a way to get to the stairs, wondering if the stairs were even safe to walk down at this point. I heard the whirr of another crane and saw Signe grab a hook, taking it as it swung up and landing on one of the platforms. She flitted across the bent paths. Signe glanced over her shoulder, then narrowed her sights on us. My grip on the rail tightened.

I grabbed Kelsy and pulled her down with me to lie on the catwalk, trying to keep her safe from any bullets. My muscles were so tense that they were growing exhausted. Signe dropped down from another path onto ours. My eyes were transfixed with horror. I covered Kelsy as best I could. She started coming towards us. My breath quickened. *Is she going to use us as hostages?* I searched everywhere for an escape. There wasn't one.

I ducked my head down and squeezed my eyes shut. A bang pierced the air. When nothing hit us, I opened one eye.

Signe fell back on the crooked platform, ducking the incoming fire. When she stood up a small box slipped out of her jacket. She jumped from our path to another one below. I searched for the reason, and spotted General Glaive outside the cover of machinery, pointing his gun at the catwalk. In a split second, my eyes met the general's, and I knew he had driven her away. He raced towards the back and my eyes followed him.

The box slid down the lopsided path. I recognized it; I knew what was in it and a mix of emotions welled up at once. I was tempted to grab it and throw it in the molten sand out of spite, but that wouldn't accomplish anything. It was still a piece of history, and as mad as I was about everything I couldn't blame it on an inanimate object.

My hand slapped on top of it when it slid nearby and I shoved it into my pocket, feeling dirty as I did.

"Sissy!" Kelsy cried. I whipped my head back around. Among the chaotic masses rumbling in the entrance, I spotted Axe. She limped heavily, barely dragging herself along, and yet she pushed through the crowd. Even in her weakened state, covered in blood and powered only by her will, no one sought out a fight with her. One man fell in her direction and I thought he would knock her over, but she braced herself and shoved him to the ground before moving on.

"Sissy, help!" Kelsy screamed for her, getting on her hands and knees. Axe's eyes turned up towards us, expression emotionless. *"I never felt anything for her,"* I repeated in my head, *She's going to leave us here.* She stared up at us, eyes glazed over. I waited for her to leave us and readied myself for her sister's confusion.

I was stunned when she took a step in our direction. She staggered over to the crooked structure and reached out a hand to touch one of the skinny support beams. I clung tighter to the grating when she lifted the axe. It bashed into the beam and broke it further, causing the whole structure to vibrate. She kept hacking at it until it gave way. I held onto Kelsy and the side as the walkway began going lopsided.

She beat down the supports until the remaining beams twisted and collapsed under the weight. Kelsy screamed as we swung down in an arc, and I may have made some sort of noise as well. The metal screeched until it finally came to a stop several feet above the floor. We were lying on the rail instead of the grate by that point, clinging onto the bars.

I helped lower Kelsy to the floor and hopped down after her. Axe stood, leaning on the hilt of the axe, looking tired. I gripped Kelsy's arm, waiting.

Axe lumbered towards the brawl ahead. Holding onto Kelsy, I skittered after her, keeping my head low. We went through the mob, staying in a safe spot directly behind Axe as she bulldozed through the crowd. We slowly inched our way outside, ducking behind her.

We snuck through the majority of the crowd. Just when we were nearly to safety she stopped. She jammed the points of her axe into the floor again and leaned on the hilt.

My eyes darted around to the people beating each other all around us. It was a terrible place to stop, but Axe wasn't moving. *Am I going to have to get Kelsy the rest of the way?* I doubted my ability to make it all the way out with her. I was too small, and not much of a fighter.

Axe's fingers tightened on the hilt and she straightened, roaring above the crowd, "Out of my way before I go through you!"

People in front of her were stricken, flailing before scuttling away from her to fight. When Axe didn't move forward, my grip tightened on Kelsy's wrist. We only had so long before the horde filled the space back up. I darted ahead, whizzing through the narrow path that had formed. We scuffled through the edge of the fight and broke away from the crowd, running into the open fields. Both of us glanced back; Axe wasn't running after us. She was still towering over the crowd.

When we got farther away, I looked back once more. I didn't see her above the masses anymore. She was gone.

I ran as far as my body would allow before ducking behind a tree and collapsing. My lungs stung after being exposed to the heat and steam inside the factory. I sat with Kelsy, recuperating.

She spoke up after a while, "Where's Sissy?"

I stayed quiet, but not because I was ignoring her like the others had. I didn't want to tell her that her sister was no longer standing.

She stood up, ready to head back, but I grabbed her and held her. "Don't go back!"

"But I have to get Sissy," she said.

"We're not strong enough to do anything." I hung on. "She wanted to get you out. Don't go back in."

I had to hold everything in and try to be strong for her. Her entire world was falling apart: her sister was a murderer; she had been in a gang of counterfeiters; her sister was dead or would be soon; and her sister wasn't even her real sister. It was a lot for a young mind to comprehend.

I wrapped an arm around her and held her, eyes turning back in the direction of all the chaos. "*I never felt anything for her,*" I thought yet again, *I wonder if that was true. She still came for her.*

Any revenge plans Axe had were abandoned, no longer possible for her.

After I recovered, I led Kelsy back towards Sundecht and hid nearby. It was a couple of hours later when the first trucks started coming. Then, in a flash, police were everywhere. The warehouse was unlocked and we watched people being led out. They weren't immediately packed into the vehicles; many seemed anxious and stood around as police coaxed them out.

The Melechtions showed up with the rest, giving directions to the police. I pointed Dorrius out to her. He was standing by the corner of the building with

Tyrus.

"He should be able to make sure you're safe. And he'll know if they recover your sister." I knew well that if they did "recover" her, they wouldn't be taking her anywhere nice, but I couldn't tell Kelsy that. I didn't know how to tell her. It would be better to let them take her to professionals who could counsel her appropriately.

She stood up, looking back at me with fear written on her face.

"It's okay," I assured her.

She turned and made her way to the group, trotting out. As she neared them, Dorrius wandered over to a group of police, directing them. My hair stood on end as I watched her approach Tyrus, but Tetchion spotted her and swept in between the two. I sighed, relieved.

He knelt by her and they spoke. Kelsy moved her hands as she talked, and Tetchion nodded to show her he was listening. They spent a few minutes before he stood up and led her to one of the trucks. He held her hand and helped her up, and stood by the back of the truck as he gestured towards the seats. It wasn't long before Kelsy left my field of vision. Tetchion climbed in after her, taking a seat next to her with his hands folded and arms resting near his knees as they continued chatting. I hadn't heard him say much during my entire time here, but I got the feeling that he was being protective.

I sagged against the tree, leaning my head back and closing my eyes.

Another truck pulled up, this one with General Glaive as a passenger. Relief washed over me seeing that he was alive and well. I listened as closely as I could to discern what happened after I left.

There was banging in the back of the truck, and screaming.

"Take all the children to be rehabilitated," Glaive told the others.

"I'll never give up!" Signe screamed from inside of the truck.

Glaive seemed not to care, answering in a monotone voice, "Then I'll see you in two years."

All around, the soldiers and officers continued speaking extensively to the hostages as they patiently worked with them.

Feeling confident about Kelsy's situation, I finally crept away. I still had one important thing to do.

I spent the rest of the day searching between where the first warehouse used to be and the town, covering as much territory as I possibly could. By the time evening came, my legs were numb and I still hadn't found a trace of Valli. I didn't want to give up and go back but I knew I had to leave at some point. The sun was going down and soon I wouldn't be able to see much anyway, so with a heart lower than the ground, I slunk back to the hotel.

I ignored the people at the counter until I heard "Dorrius" in their chatter. I immediately stopped and went over.

"What's going on?" I asked.

"Dorrius showed up here earlier. Can you

believe that?"

"What did he want?"

"He wanted to go into one of the rooms. It was strange, but he was probably here less than twenty minutes before he left with some kids."

Loren and Merrian.

"Were they scared?" I asked.

She shook her head. "Didn't look like it. There was a tiny one holding his hand and another one following him."

I nodded and left, heading up to my room.

I searched the bedroom, the bathing room, and the bathroom. Both kids were gone, undoubtedly picked up. As I walked to the bed, I caught sight of something on the dresser. A picture of two stick figures was scratched into it, one a little taller with long hair and a smaller one with short hair. They stood side-by-side with their little stick arms touching. I traced my finger over the drawing. They were gone and I wasn't going to see them again.

I tossed the box with the necklace onto the edge of the bed and plopped down. After all that, I hadn't found Valli. I buried myself in the sheets.

When I glanced up, I noticed a message was left on the phone. *Dad.* I took a deep breath and dragged myself to the v-phone, pulling up the message.

I was stunned into silence. An image of Valli popped up. He was lying on a bed with a lightweight gown on.

"Hi ... Leander," his voice sounded wistful,

tired. "Ah, sorry I didn't call sooner. I'm at the hospital, whenever you get back."

The message ended there. I brushed aside everything else and jumped to my feet, bolting out of the hotel and getting on the first cart to the hospital. I ran straight to the counter.

"May I help you?" the receptionist asked.

"I'm here to see Valli. Is he here?" I couldn't believe his message. I needed to confirm that he was truly there. She gave me directions and I rushed to the elevator, getting myself lost in my haste. I wandered the oddly numbered rooms until I found my way, peeking into Valli's room.

He was resting on the bed with his hands folded in front of him. The room had a pattern of light blue flowers painted around it, with a dresser by the bed and a couple of chairs. I could hardly believe my eyes. I had believed so strongly that he was dead. How did he get here?

I sat next to his bed, debating whether or not to wake him. Finally I nudged him gently and he stirred awake, staring at me groggily.

"Oh, Leander ..." he yawned.

"Valli ... I can't believe you're alive. I've been looking for you everywhere! What happened? The last time I saw you was outside that warehouse." I had so many questions.

He stared blankly at me for a moment as he seemed to process what I said. "I'm sorry. I would have called sooner but I was unconscious ..." He sat up straighter, waking up more. "They had to put me out for a while so they could operate."

"How did you get here?"

"Well, after you left, I knew I needed to get to the hospital ... So I snuck back into the warehouse and took that truck you turned on. I ... I didn't really know how to drive it, but I managed to get back to the city." He winced at the memory. "It was so bumpy and horrible ... I threw up all over the front."

He sounded so regretful that I couldn't help but smile at him. "It's fine. The people who had to clean it up deserved it anyway."

"When I got back to the city, I didn't think I would make it, but some people there spotted me and helped get me to the hospital. They had to knock me out so they could fix me up and ... well, since they were operating anyway, they did my surgery, too. I'm sorry I didn't call sooner."

I took his hand, holding it up as I leaned over his bed. My forehead was nearly touching it. "Don't worry about it." I was so relieved that I didn't care. I was just so glad to see him okay.

I still wasn't positive what his surgery was, but that did remind me of something.

"Hey, Valli. When I left you there you already had bandages on, but you said you didn't have anything done yet, so what were they for?"

He stared up at me, looking a little uncertain, but finally answered, "I just used them to keep everything ... strapped down. I won't need them anymore."

It was confusing but if he didn't want to

elaborate that was fine with me.

I squeezed his hand in mine. "I'm so glad you're okay."

He smiled back with a chuckle, then yawned. "Sorry, I've been feeling a little lightheaded because of the medications. It's been hard to think clearly. And I've been so drowsy …"

"Don't worry. I'll take care of everything. Go ahead and rest."

He sat up a bit longer before slumping back down and quickly drifting away. I lingered around in the room for the extra confirmation that he was definitely there; he was okay.

When I left to go back to the hotel, I felt lighter. I kept repeating it in my head: *Valli is okay.* After days of feeling hopeless it was hard to believe. As soon as I got back to the hotel I was ready to relax, when I looked at the phone again. Talking to my dad sounded like a good idea.

But first I needed a wash. Bad. I filled the tub with warm water and got in, lying back and letting my body go limp. I let the water permeate my skin.

I breathed in the steam, and was almost ready to fall asleep when I heard the v-phone beeping. *Dad!* I didn't want to miss my opportunity to talk to him. I jumped out of the tub, grabbed a towel and wrapped it around me as I rushed back into the other room.

Plopping on the chair, I turned on the v-phone.

"Hello, Leander," Dad replied before he got a good look at me. I had a towel wrapped around my waist, but the v-phone only showed my bust, and I was dripping. I wasn't worried about him, of course, but I heard whistles coming from his side of the v-phone. He glanced to the side with an irritated glare. "Shut up, that's my son!"

Ever protective, he launched a pillow off screen at someone. Laughter drowned out the whistling as he staved off his fellow soldiers.

I grinned at him, not worried about the other people. "Hi Dad."

"Put on something," he ordered me, hand covering half his face.

I laughed and wrapped the towel over my shoulders. They wouldn't be able to see below my waist anyway. "I was just taking a bath."

"What's going on?"

I had specific things I wanted to talk about for once. I brushed my hair back, searching for the words. "Valli is okay. I just visited him at the hospital."

"That's good to hear."

I bit my lip, leaning back and folding my arms. "I managed to leave a message about the kids. Dorrius came and got them, but … do you think they'll keep them together?"

He mulled it over. "It depends. Someone will have to decide if it's best for them to stay together. But you did the right thing."

"Yeah …" I wasn't as certain. I hated to think of them possibly being separated, but I had to do it. "You think they'll be okay?"

"Of course they'll be okay. We look after our own, and you can hardly get better help than that," he answered confidently, then changed the subject, "Do you know when you'll be heading back home yet?"

"Oh." I blinked in surprise. "Not yet. I was just so relieved." I let out a small, dry laugh. "I forgot to ask."

Dad smiled softly, "Make sure to let me know when you find out."

I nodded.

We had a short chat that included another bout of him yelling at the other soldiers before he had to go.

I stayed by the v-phone and looked up information about orphanages to ease my mind. I learned that the most children a qualified caretaker could have at once was eight, and if they had more than four they needed an assistant in training with them, or two. The pictures I skimmed through showed art rooms and gardening centers and play areas. At nineteen they would start a two-year transitional period and get help finding a job and new place to live. It wasn't the same as having a family, I decided, but they should be able to make it.

I found an article about a couple who decided to become caretakers after learning they couldn't have children and let the positivity take me in. Even if it wasn't a family, they'd have live-in, trained professionals who would know how to handle them, and perhaps, one day, they would get adopted.

I finally shut it down and collapsed on the bed. The picture carved onto the dresser caught my eye. I'd have to pay for that, but I hardly had the strength to care.

15

The next day, I checked on Valli. I fidgeted relentlessly; after the last few days, it was weird not having something to do. General Glaive appeared on the news, explaining that there had been a mistaken report in our area. It at least proved to Dad that I hadn't been making stuff up.

Dad had the brightest smile when I told him we'd be heading back home the next morning. I made sure to stop by for another bowl of clam chowder, and rested up until the next morning when I helped Valli get ready and we waited for our ride. It was still dark, and I was surprised when a hovercraft showed up.

"You said that you were disappointed it wasn't a hovercraft the first time ..." Valli began. I didn't give him time to explain before climbing aboard.

It was a small one with enough room for us. Our luggage would be delivered later. Even though I was tired from waking up early, I ran back and forth between the windows to get a view of the world whizzing by. Normally we'd be taking a nap until we got to our destination, but with a hovercraft we'd go so fast that it would only be a couple hours to get back. I'd have to catch up on my sleep later.

When we got back I helped him get to the theater, which was surprisingly empty. He explained everyone was out doing a lot of promotion.

I didn't intend to wait around. After Valli was

safely home I headed to the bar.

Even if I'd never gotten along with Galloughs, seeing him scrubbing up was a welcome relief compared to what I'd been through. I approached the bar, tired and impatient.

"I need to see Ellora," I stated.

"You look frazzled."

"You have no idea what I've been through the past few days."

"Being a little dramatic?"

"Dramatic? I've been neck deep in murderers who had spies everywhere," I ranted, pausing in consideration. "Then again, one of their members was a spy for the army, too."

"That's how spies work. They get in there and blend in, sometimes for years. For all I know you could be a spy." he cocked an eyebrow at me suspiciously as he wiped the counter.

"I'm not a spy!" I huffed.

"That's exactly what a spy would say."

I glared at him before a thought struck me. A smirked worked its way across my face. "I can't be a spy. I'm eighteen. The government doesn't hire minors."

He remained silent, his eyes meeting mine briefly before reluctantly giving in. "Fair enough."

Victory was mine.

"Ha ha!" I celebrated, only to fall into a coughing fit.

He lost focus on his work, stopping to ask more

softly, "Something wrong?"

The coughing prevented me from responding immediately, so I waved my hand dismissively, sputtering out what I could while covering my mouth with my arm, "I'm fine … I was j-just exposed to some smoke for awhile."

After watching me struggle, he filled up a glass and set it in front of me with a clonk. I raised my brows, not used to being anything besides antagonistic with him, before chugging it down. I still had a prickling sensation inside my chest, but the water quelled it for the time being.

There was an awkward silence after I finished it, and I ended up quietly going to the back room to wait for Ellora.

When she showed, I needed only to pop open the box and I had her full attention.

"Apparently, it had paperwork to authenticate it, but I don't have any of that," I told her.

"That's fine. I'll just take it to Pirion to get it authenticated." She reached out to take it and I pulled it away.

"I went through way too much to get this. *I'll* take it to Pirion."

I was determined not to let her take advantage of me this time.

"I don't have time for this, I have a performance to do tonight," she complained.

"Then you'll have to hurry up and show me how to get there." I stayed firm.

I didn't budge, and finally, she conceded. A sprig of joy grew in me. I hadn't let her push me around, and I was finally going to learn where one of the entrances to the black market was.

We took a cart all the way to the edge of the city, where she led me into the woods north of the capital. Much of it was protected, but paths were still made through it.

On the way we passed a strange structure. The wall surrounding it must have been around twenty feet high, but many of the structures inside were much taller than the wall. It had a high tower and looked to be some sort of mish-mash between a huge mansion and a small, interconnected town. Dull grays shaded the whole thing, and the way much of it was chipped away and looked decrepit reminded me of Wilten Crags.

"What's that?"

Ellora stopped to look over, furrowing her brows.

"No one knows for sure. People think it's something General Glaive made, though. It only popped up in the last two years."

The General made it?

"Then why does it look so *old*?" I asked.

"I don't know."

"What's it for?"

"*I don't know*," she answered sharply. "A lot of people have asked about getting stuff out of there," she glanced back at me and shrugged, "but I have a bad feeling about that place, so I told them no."

"I'm glad to hear you have some sort of standards for where you'll send me," I quipped.

As we continued forward I glanced back at the building between the trees. *Maybe General Glaive isn't completely misunderstood.*

She led me to a cave in the woods and took me inside. The tunnels were deceptively long and forked in many areas, but after a lengthy walk, I heard the unmistakable chatter of the crowd.

As we walked into the black market I realized how long it had been. I looked around in awe, yet again. I remembered Pirion being around the middle. I stood before the rows of endless goods, eyes roaming the area.

"Well," Ellora folded her arms, "don't you know what to do?"

I gave her a dazed look. "Don't I just give this to Pirion?"

She huffed, "You have no style."

I quirked a brow at her. "Then what would *you* do?"

She snatched the box from my hand. "Watch and learn."

She strutted into the market with full confidence, but she didn't head straight for Pirion. Instead she went to a shop that seemed mostly empty, striking a conversation with the owner.

"What's going on, Foleshian?"

"I haven't gotten my shipment yet. The government went and shut them down. I've barely got anything to sell," the owner griped.

"They're always getting in the way." She wrinkled her nose. "But I think you'll like what I've got, then." Ellora wagged the box in front of her.

She kicked a rolling chair to the pathway and jumped on top of it, announcing loudly, "Ladies and gentlemen! I know you're tired of the government going after your businesses. I present to you," she opened the box and held up the necklace in all its glory, "the necklace of the late king himself! Taken from right under their noses!"

She was drawing all sorts of attention. Behind me, two women and a man were whispering to each other.

"How does she manage to get stuff like that?"

"I have no idea."

"And she's so famous, too."

I watched her make a spectacle of herself as she played to the crowd.

"Do you think they'd notice it if I wore it during one of our plays?" she joked, putting the necklace on and doing a short, overly dramatic mockery of a love song, throwing an arm to her forehead as she fell back in the chair. I would have felt like an idiot doing something like that, but people were laughing and clapping. She was completely playing to their tastes, making fun of the government.

When she was done she bowed and made one last announcement, "And go buy some bags from Foleshian. She didn't get her new merchandise so she might as well sell what's left of what she's got so she can go home."

I picked up one of Foleshian's bags, looking it over. Although it looked fine from a distance, on the inside I saw the uneven stitching. It reminded me far too much of another bag I'd seen recently. I frowned and put it down. I wouldn't be shopping around here.

Ellora began marching to Pirion. It took me a moment before I jogged after her. I followed a bit behind her until we got there, feeling a little nervous. I didn't want to be in the spotlight like that.

"What was all that about?" I whispered to her.

"It's called socializing," she snapped. "You don't get information by sitting in a dark corner by yourself."

She put the necklace away and slapped the box down on the counter. "I need to get this appraised."

Pirion moved closer, putting on a pair of latex gloves before picking it up and examining it. "Oh, this is very nice …"

"I need to get it authenticated and I need to know how much it's worth," Ellora told her bluntly. Pirion examined it, turning it over and holding it up quizzically before nodding.

"Certainly. But it'll be a few hours."

"Hmm, I've got somewhere I need to be." She tapped my shoulder. "But you don't have anything going on. You can wait here."

I glared at her. I didn't much care for that assumption, but I wasn't in the mood to argue. Ellora left while Pirion was still looking over the necklace.

"So what do you think?" I asked. She studied it

closely.

"It's good. It's very good … but I need to take a closer look at it. There seems to be something on it, too."

"There is?" I looked at it, but it just looked shiny to me.

"Hmm, yes." She pulled out a small swab, wiping a tiny spot as if she was double checking. "I need to use some better equipment. I'll be back in a couple hours."

"Sure."

Although I was irritated, it wasn't at Pirion. It wasn't at much of anyone directly. I was just tired. As soon as she left I took a seat by the counter and folded my arms on it, resting my head on top of them.

I drifted off a few times before she finally came back. I noticed her because she was running, which seemed odd for her, so I looked up.

When she came closer I asked, "Is it real?"

She shook her head. "No, it's a counterfeit. A very good counterfeit, but a fake nonetheless." She seemed a little out of breath.

All that trouble for a necklace that wasn't even the real thing. I felt even more aggravated than before, but there was some satisfaction at the idea that the counterfeiters had been fooled by a counterfeit.

"More importantly, did you ever touch this necklace?" she asked.

I cocked my head. I held the box plenty of times but I didn't recall taking the necklace out. "No, I don't think so ..."

"Good. It seems to be covered in poison."

I straightened up quickly. "Poison? What kind?"

"I'm not positive the exact details. All I can tell is it's a slow acting one that clots the blood. If you touched it you can go get treated at the hospital and be fine."

"I'm pretty sure I didn't ..." I scanned my memory.

Lieran! That's how he died. It suddenly made sense. Signe had made sure he touched the necklace. Then I recalled that the gang had paperwork to authenticate it, and didn't seem to think it was a fake. "Wait, how do you know it's a fake?"

"Well, it's a very good fake, mind you, but the original necklace was very old, and this necklace was made with more modern techniques," she explained. "They simply wouldn't have existed back then."

I furrowed my brows. *Then how did they have paperwo* -- I stopped mid-thought as I came to a realization, *Iona was the one who found it. If the government could make a fake news report, they could easily make a fake necklace and paperwork.*

It was strange to think of so much deceit happening.

"It's a fake, but the jewels are still real. It could still be worth a little bit of money." She attempted to comfort me.

"How much?"

"Maybe a few thousand."

Which would then be split with Ellora. It wasn't nearly enough to be worth what I'd gone through. I wasn't sure anything was.

I let out a sigh, "I'm going to go to the hospital just in case." As I pushed myself out of the seat I was suddenly pinged. "Ellora!"

I didn't recall touching the necklace, but Ellora definitely had.

"Pirion, how long does that poison take to be effective?"

"I'm not sure. A few hours? It's absorbed through the skin."

I left the box behind and ran out. It didn't matter; I just had to get to Ellora before it killed her.

The only tunnel I was familiar with led to the forest. I went as fast as I could, sprinting through the cave, to the city edge and hopping on a cart at the closest spot. It felt like it took forever and my body wanted to explode, but I finally arrived at the theater. I knew Ellora's room was the last one in the row, so I picked up a rock and threw it at the window. No answer. I tried a few more times with no luck.

Valli. Valli stayed in the room next to her. I ran over and tossed a rock at his window a few times. After a minute he answered, peeking out in surprise.

"Leander?"

"Hurry, I need in!"

I climbed up the cement pot in front of his window. He seemed confused but opened it, taking my hand and helping to pull me in before sitting on the edge of his bed, placing an arm over his chest.

He chuckled softly. "People might get the wrong idea if they see you sneaking into my room like this."

I didn't mind but I had no time to joke around. "Where's Ellora?"

"Oh, she's out promoting the theater. What's going on?"

"I think she's been poisoned. Do you know where she's at?"

"Poisoned ...?" He looked at me quizzically.

"Yes, something she picked up was covered in poison. I need to find her before it kills her!"

"Ah ... She's outside the castle. But there will be a large crowd and security. You'll have a hard time getting close to her." He furrowed his brows. "Are you certain?"

"I am!"

Just as he stood up I climbed back out the window and ran to the closest cart. The castle was a big place and there were several stops near it. I picked one near the central entrance so that I could go any direction I needed.

It was easy to spot when I got there. To the right of the castle, there was a large crowd of people and a stage set up. I made a mad dash out of the cart. I could make out some people performing on the stage, dancing and singing. When I reached the crowd, I was caught in a forest of people.

I pushed through, mumbling some "Excuse me"s as I went. As I got closer to the front I saw Ellora on the stage along with some dancers. The crowd got more difficult to force my way through. I had to jab my arms through and pry my way between.

I stumbled as I reached the front, looking up at the stage. Ellora was in the center, belting out a song, completely unaware of me.

"Ellora!" I tried to yell as loud as I could but it was no good with all the noise. "Ellora!"

I moved my way to the side, looking to get away from the thickest part of the crowd in front of the stage. Once I found a spot where the crowd was thinner I grabbed the side of the stage, pulling myself up. I spotted the pink jackets of the guards coming after me immediately. I didn't have time. I yanked myself up and stumbled forward, running straight to Ellora as they climbed up.

"Ellora!" I ran up to her and grabbed her arm.

Her ears tilted down as I interrupted her, lowering the microphone as she asked me, "What are you doing here?"

The guards were already on the stage making their way towards us. I tried to get out everything I could. "Ellora, you're poisoned. You need to go to the hospital!"

"What are you talking about?" she growled under her breath.

The guards grabbed my arms and pulled on me. I held onto her as tightly as I could. "The necklace was covered in poison! If you don't get to the hospital your blood will clot!"

She stared at me as the guards overpowered me and dragged me away. They were too strong, I couldn't break away. It was only then I heard all the noise from the anxious crowd. Her eyes were puzzled; the entire performance was brought to a halt while I was pulled off the stage.

As I hoped that she heard me, that she would listen to me and tried to tug out of the guards' grip I watched her raise a hand to her forehead and collapse. My eyes widened as I tried to lunge forward but was held back. "Ellora!"

The crowd erupted in a stunned roar of gasps and shouts. Other guards ran by and climbed onto the stage. Dancers around her stepped back to give them space, watching in a stunned silence, clueless what to do.

A guard knelt by her, checking her and shouting something to the other guard. I could only watch. I had been too late.

Emergency medical staff arrived and carried her off to a hospital cart as guards kept a path clear for them to get through.

I turned to the guards holding me. They didn't know what was wrong with her; I needed to tell them.

"She was poisoned!" I told them. "It'll make her blood clot. The doctors need to know what it is!"

They wrestled with me to keep me in place. It seemed like I was never going to get anywhere until in all the chaos there was suddenly Valli. He was using a cane and hobbling as he held his chest. He was already next to us before I spotted him, placing a hand on one of the guard's arms to get her attention.

"It's okay. He's with me," he told her. I waited as

he talked to them, until they finally let go of me.

I paused by Valli, practically bouncing in place, ready to burst. "They need to know what's wrong."

"Go, go," he told me. With one last restless hop I ran at top speeds to take a cart to the hospital.

Hours later, I sat on a hospital bed, glaring at the bed across from me.

Ellora was sitting on it, looking perky.

I felt lightheaded from the medicine, but I preferred to deal with the side effects and be certain that I wouldn't have any clots. I informed them that I had been exposed to smoke while I was there, and they had examined and treated me. I was fortunate enough that I wasn't seriously injured.

"I can't believe you pretended to faint," I muttered. She'd frightened me, as well as hundreds of other people – if not thousands.

"Eh, it was the fastest way to get to the hospital. Besides, it'll be quite a story when people are reading the news," she answered lightly.

I came to the hospital to get treated and check on her, but knowing she was fine and had faked being ill, I didn't feel like staying there at all. Luckily, Valli showed up not long after that.

I threw my legs over the side of the bed to go as he walked in.

"Oh, you're going?" he asked, seeming disappointed.

"Yeah, I'm tired. I'm heading home."

"All right … Take care."

Exhausted and dizzy, I finally went home, ready to collapse on my bed and get some sleep.

Bonus

When I got home, the luggage wasn't in front of my house yet. *It still hasn't arrived?* I was too exhausted to even worry about it.

When I opened the door, Dad was standing in the living room, carrying a bundle of sheets in his arms.

"Dad!" I shouted. I flew by the luggage just inside the door and clung onto him like feathers on a bird.

"Leander." He wrapped an arm around me, maneuvering to keep the blankets from falling on the floor.

I couldn't contain my excitement when I asked, "What are you doing here?"

"I wanted to surprise you, but you were out." He squeezed my shoulder then lifted the blankets. "So I thought I'd do some chores that you've probably put off."

My lip twitched up at the corner. I couldn't remember the last time I'd washed my sheets, although I was sure I'd done it at some point.

"Uh, yeah, some stuff came up with my friend so I stuck around a little longer," I explained, wishing I'd known he was home.

"Well, at least you're here now." His voice became more questioning as he continued, "Although I am curious what happened to the garden."

"The garden ...?"

Panic jolted through me at the thought of what he meant. I darted to the back door and flung it open. There in front of me sat the garden, thoroughly dug up. The only plant left was our single fruit tree.

"There was a lympet ..." I weakly tried to explain.

"Honestly, I'm surprised you didn't try to draw some pictures of fruits and stick them in the ground to cover it up," he replied with good humor.

"*Dad*. I was only seven when that happened."

I was an adult now. I wouldn't try to do something silly like draw a picture of a branch and tape it to a tree. I'd at least sculpt some models out of paper.

As faced him I let out a sigh. "Sorry, I wasn't able to stop it."

"It's okay. I know you were gone," he spoke softly, but hardened as he continued, "But I need to talk to you about something else. Your teachers have said you've been missing school."

I froze. There had been days I had skipped in order to go find stuff. With Dad gone it had been easier to do without getting caught, but with him talking to my teachers ... I lowered my ears. "I just got busy."

"Did you even know you have a history test coming up?"

I glanced to the side. I didn't. I hadn't really worried about it.

He sighed. "You're going to have to study."

I stared at him. I didn't want to be stuck home

studying, especially not while he was here. I needed some way, any way, to get out of it. "But I can't study now. You're here!"

"I'm going to help you study," he answered firmly.

"But that's no fun!"

"You should have thought about that before you started skipping classes."

"But you can't be staying for very long!"

"I leave tomorrow night, and if you have to study the entire time then so be it."

My mind screamed not to give in. I didn't want to spend the whole time studying, especially not the entire time I had with my dad. I needed a good excuse, and for once I came up with something.

"But I have tickets!"

"Hmm?"

"Valli gave me tickets to the theater. They're really expensive, so we shouldn't waste them."

"I don't know about that, Leander ..."

"Come on, you wouldn't have to cook anything for dinner, and we could see a show, and I don't know when I'll get to see you again!" I piled it on, giving him the big eyes.

He stayed quiet before shaking his head. "All right. But the rest of the time you're studying. Don't even try to get out of it."

I brightened up instantly. He got me to sit down and study for a little bit before we needed to get ready for the theater.

"I don't have much in the way of fancy clothes," I muttered when he came up to my room in one of his finer uniforms. The army had a few options. It was common for soldiers to have a few of the fancier ones around since they wore them out so often.

"You can use one of my uniforms," he offered.

I bounded down the stairs to go into his closet, pulling out one of the uniforms. Dad came down after I put on the jacket and dress pants. They were too big on me when I looked in the mirror.

"This is your fault," I told him.

"What is?"

"I'm short."

He cocked a brow at me. "You didn't get that from me. Blame your mother."

"You married someone short. If you married someone tall I'd be taller."

"I didn't fall in love with someone tall ..." he murmured under his breath.

I pinned the pants up and we were off. The theater was crowded, as expected of the most famous theater in the country. I hadn't spent much time inside of it before. The lobby was huge and well furnished with lots of places to sit and relax. Shops lined the side of the lobby. We followed the crowd and figured our way out as we explored.

"You know, we had a little theater where I grew up, but they didn't have the type of actors they get here. Some were good, some weren't so good," he told me. "They had this gimmick where they would sometimes change the way a play ended or something, so you could go see the same show twice and it would be different each time. It was fun."

I listened as he reminisced. "Did you go to shows a lot?"

"More often than I did here. It wasn't as expensive, though. And I had fewer bills to pay."

"I don't remember you ever coming here."

"Ryki took me once. That was about it."

The topic of our conversation didn't matter. I was just glad to have him there. Talking to him face to face again was incredible.

People were ushered into the theater. When I showed my ID, we were escorted to the second floor and led to balcony seats. The seats were cushy and had a table in front of them with menus. I browsed the menu, flipping through the options before clicking what I wanted and relaxing.

It was strange watching the show. It was the first time I'd seen Ellora act, and she wasn't a background character like she had been in the first script I'd seen. She was playing a lead role as a singer, and she was a good singer. I was surprised she was performing so soon after going to the hospital. She was stubborn, though.

I had to admit she was talented. We watched the show, enjoyed the holograms that drifted around us when it was supposed to be snowing in the play, and felt the cold wind shoot out to complete the experience. The food was delicious and I was completely immersed in the experience by the end.

After the show people started pouring into the

lobby. I waited in my seat with Dad to let the crowd disperse before trying to fight our way through. After most left their seats, I grabbed my dad and went to the lower floor, holding his hand as I took him down the aisle and towards the stage.

"Come on, I'll introduce you," I told him.

When most had left we arrived at the stage and I climbed up, ushering him after me. I headed straight for the curtains I'd been behind before. Ellora was standing there, and I spotted Valli hiding behind the curtains in a chair.

"Ellora!"

A guard approached, but when Ellora glanced over she quickly waved her off and came over to me.

"Don't tell me you joined the army."

I glanced down at my outfit. "No, this is my dad's." I looked behind me. "And this is my dad. Dad, this is Ellora."

He extended a hand. "Pleased to meet you."

It was strange seeing Ellora be polite, shaking his hand firmly. "Good to meet you, too."

I grabbed him to pull him further along. "And this is Valli."

Valli nodded his head lightly. "Sorry, I would stand but I'm not feeling well."

"That's fine." My dad took his hand; "My boy told me that you had some difficulties. I'm glad to see you're okay."

Valli smiled softly. "Thank you. Did you enjoy the show?"

"I did. I haven't been to the theater in a long time."

"You'll have to come again sometime. We're always putting on new shows."

I sat on a bar next to him and had a long conversation before Dad and I headed home.

When we were on the way, my dad had a strange smile on his face. "I get it now."

"Get what?"

"I see why you're slacking off at school." He nodded. "But you need to think about your future. She has a good job. She won't be interested if you don't do something with yourself."

I boggled about what he was talking about before it clicked. "What?" I couldn't even imagine being interested in Ellora, and if Dad knew her better, he wouldn't want me to be. "I don't like her!"

"I was around your age when I met your mother."

"I'm not interested in her. At all," I informed him. I could only imagine how horrendous that relationship would be. Ellora didn't seem the type to be interested in any sort of relationship. She had too much going on and she didn't want to give anything up.

As soon as we got home Dad made me study. I lay on the couch while he sat on a chair nearby with a history book.

And it was completely, utterly boring. As he read I groaned loudly and clutched my chest, rolling over onto my stomach and pressing my face into the cushions, arms wrapped around my head.

"... So during the scientific revolution, which ruler was it who established that there should be a balance between nature, science and the unknown?"

From my spot I muffled out, "This is so boring, it's painful." After a moment I peeked out from under my arm.

My dad grabbed my ear and lifted it up. "Which ruler?"

"King Lariat?" I groaned. He seemed as good a guess as any.

"Queen Lambrian," he informed me bluntly. "You take the system we have for granted. Back then it was a big deal. People were constantly discovering new things. Some people thought the new technology was evil and some thought it was the only way to progress. Queen Lambrian made it okay to advance technology, but she also acknowledged the importance of nature."

I let out a lengthy groan to express my discontent.

"Which general murdered the king?"

"King Lariat?" I guessed again. He could have been alive hundreds of years ago, been a general and a woman, so why not?

He pinched me for being smart and corrected me. "General Luenlore."

He continued on about how the modern royal bloodline wasn't related to the bloodline of the olden days.

I grabbed my chest. "I think I'm having a heart attack!"

"You're not having a heart attack."

"I'm losing all feeling."

"Knock it off." He nudged my side with his foot. "Why is it that you love mystery novels, but you hate learning about the assassination of a real king?"

"Because history classes take all the excitement out of it. There's no tension!" I bolted up. "If I was teaching a history class I'd make everyone solve who did it!"

"That's a great idea." He glanced back at the book. "You can do that once you learn your history. So pay attention."

He kept me there the rest of the day, studying the entire time. I was relieved when evening came and we started getting ready for bed.

After I took my bath and headed up to my room I paused on the stairway to peek down at him.

He glanced up at me from the couch. "What is it?"

"Aren't you going to tuck me in?"

"I haven't tucked you in since you were a boy." He chuckled.

"What, afraid you can't make it up the stairs anymore?"

He took the quip as a challenge and I ran upstairs to my room with him close behind. I lunged onto my bed, rolling over to face him. Dad had no trouble keeping up, walking in just behind me. He had the same look on his face as he usually did when he thought I was being strange: a grin with a quizzical look in his eyes, but he went along with it without complaint.

He lifted the edge of the cover and I slipped myself under it, lying down as he tucked it in and gave it a soft pat. Then he leaned over and kissed my forehead, just like he used to do. My smile couldn't get any bigger.

After a quiet moment, he sat down on the edge of my bed.

Uh-oh. This is going to be awkward.

"I need to talk to you," he started, hands folded in front of him.

I felt a vague sense of dread.

"I know the last year has been hard on you. But I'm not sure you understand how important your education is. What you do now will set you up for the future."

"I know, Dad. I'm fine," I answered as confidently as I could.

"I don't know about that. You never did things like skip school while I was at home." He sighed. "But you need to think about what you're going to do."

I tried to think of something encouraging to say, but only excuses came to mind. "Some of the classes are boring. That's all."

"I know it can be overwhelming. You've had to do a lot on your own, and I'm proud of you. You need to go to class and do your work, though." He paused. I wasn't sure what to say, but he continued, "If you need some help, I could always ask Ryki to come by sometimes. To give you a hand."

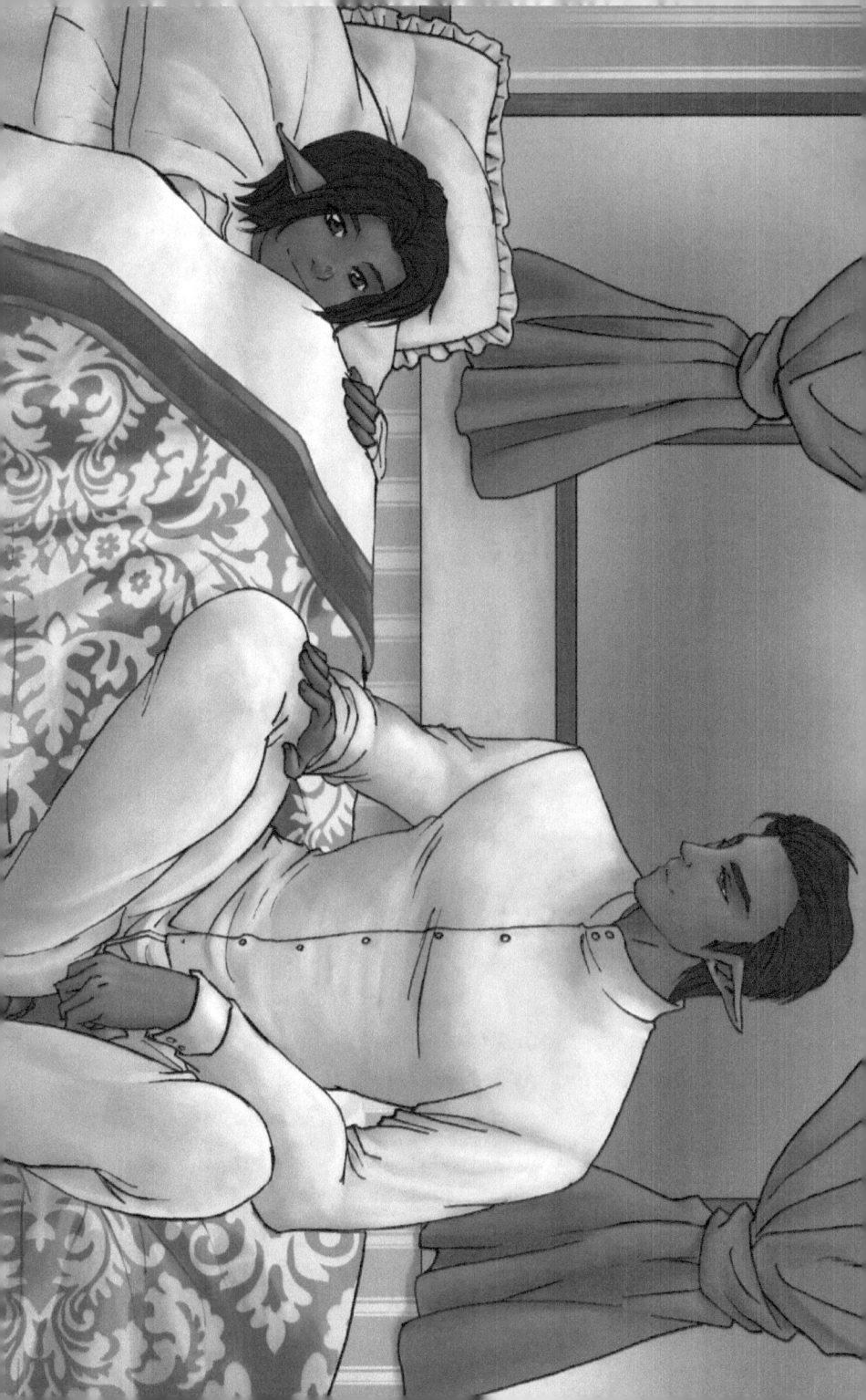

I liked Rykiel, but I didn't want him to know what I was doing any more than I wanted my dad to know. In a way I wished I could tell him what was really going on, but that would just worry him more. Maybe if I ever became a famous treasure hunter, he would understand.

"I'm fine. Really, you don't need to worry so much," I tried to reassure him.

"You know you can talk to me if something is wrong, right?"

A small pang pierced my heart.

"I know. Everything's been going great." I smiled at him. "Honest."

If only I could tell him I was trying to live out my dream, and not that I was having a life crisis. But I couldn't tell him. There was too much questionable activity involved and he'd put an end to it all.

He was watching me, possibly waiting for me to admit to anything. "Can you promise me that you'll take it more seriously?"

"I promise."

I would still have to miss some days of school while I was on a mission, but I could do more.

After a moment of silence he accepted the answer and patted my leg, standing up. "Well, I should get some sleep. Can you move all right?"

I wiggled around under the covers, "Yeah."

"Better fix that." He moved to tighten the covers.

"No!" I pushed him away as he threatened to trap me. We playfully wrestled until he backed off, heading to his room.

I was restless that night. No matter how much I tried to rest, my mind kept racing and I found myself on my feet. I neared my door and stopped. I wanted to head downstairs and jump on his bed, like I used to do, but he'd had a long trip down. He was probably exhausted and needed sleep.

Going back to sit on the edge of my bed, I kicked my feet. I spent the majority of the night fidgeting around in my room until I finally collapsed.

When I woke up, Dad was shaking my shoulder. I'd ended up falling asleep half on, half off, the bed. I mumbled some gibberish and looked up at him.

Fully dressed and ready to go, he smiled brightly at me. "I'm heading out for my jog."

The usual morning jog. He liked to keep in shape.

"I'll come!" I popped up, finding a burst of energy hidden somewhere inside of me. I got dressed and we were off in the chill of the morning, despite doctor's orders that I should rest.

Attempting to out-do him, I ran as fast as I could down the street. It didn't take long for me to tire out, and soon he was jogging past me and I was struggling to keep up. He ended his jog sooner than I expected – I was sure it was for me – and we went home for more studying time.

Next thing I knew I was being shaken awake.

When I looked up, Dad was there in his uniform and his bag slung over his shoulder, crouching next to the couch. Outside, the sky was already purple.

"It's time for me to go."

I rolled off the couch to my feet.

"Wait! I want to go, too." I rushed to grab my jacket and some shoes.

"All right. We can have dinner on the ride there."

I hurried after him, flustered. "You could have woken me up!"

"You conked out like a newborn. I figured you must have needed the sleep," he explained.

"I didn't mean to leave you alone all day, though."

Nor had I intended to miss my time with him.

"It's fine. Ryki came over and we went out on the porch and talked for a while," he consoled me.

"Rykiel came over?" I cried louder than I meant to.

"For a bit."

I had missed Dad *and* Rykiel. If only I hadn't lost so much sleep in the last week.

We boarded a dining cart that was otherwise empty. I wanted to say something to him but I didn't know what to talk about. We stood in front of the selection of food at the front of the cart. My eyes trailed down to a pastry at the bottom, brightly decorated with fresh fruits.

"You have to eat dinner first." My dad's voice interrupted my thoughts.

"I know, I know."

We picked our meals and sat opposite each other.

While we ate I awkwardly started the conversation, "So ... when are you going to come back?"

He sighed lightly. "I'm going to try and get a day off for your birthday and your graduation."

My birthday would be soon. Then graduation.

As I mulled it over, my dad smiled softly. "You know, I actually had something to tell you."

My ears perked up. "You did?"

"I'm going to be promoted to lieutenant." Although his smile was reserved I could see the glimmer of excitement in his eyes.

"Really?" I smiled. "It's about time! It's only been 18 years."

"To be fair, I've only been in the field for a year. But I'm sure they took into account my years of service." He rested an arm on the table as he spoke. "I should be learning to drive soon."

"Really?!" I was surprised since not many people learned to drive. "Then maybe you can drive yourself here next time!"

He chuckled. "I certainly hope not. It's about a ten hour trip."

"So when are you getting the promotion?"

"When I get back."

"Are you getting a raise, too?"

"A bit."

I knew Dad would understate whatever he was getting, but whatever it was, he was happy, and that made me happy.

When we reached the edge of the city, the truck to take Dad back to camp was waiting. We went to stand by it while we waited for everyone to show up. Down the street, another soldier was saying his good-byes to his wife and two daughters. I couldn't be sure from here but they looked like twins.

"Want to see inside?" Dad lifted the back door. The inside was simple. Four beds, arranged like bunk beds on either side. With my hands on the edge of the truck I leaned inside.

"That one is mine." He pointed at one of the top beds. I climbed into the back of the truck and pulled myself up on the bed. It was no luxury hotel, but it would do for a trip.

Wrapping myself up in the covers I peeked out at him. "I'm ready to go."

He smiled softly.

I got out of the bed and we sat on the back of the truck. The other soldier had finished hugging his family and was heading towards us.

"Lorough!" he called out with a hand in the air to greet him.

My dad responded just as enthusiastically with a wave, "Hershane!"

Hershane and Dad shook hands. Dad patted me on the shoulder. "This is my boy, Leander."

"Nice to meet you." He reached for my hand. "Your dad is a good man, I don't know what we'd do without him. Work hard and I'm sure you can be just like him."

242

"Yeah," I answered vaguely with a smile. Not that I didn't admire my dad. I did. He was everything Nagdecht could ever hope for in a citizen, but we were very different people. I didn't think I could ever be like my dad.

"Well, I'm going to settle in." He climbed into the truck, turning back for a second to salute my dad. "Lieutenant."

"I'm not a lieutenant quite yet," he corrected him with a grin.

We waited for the two other soldiers to show up. I sat on the end of the truck, legs kicking as he stood patiently by my side.

When the last of the four climbed out of a cart down the street, a sense of disappointment built up in me. We didn't have much time left.

"Well," my dad took a deep breath, "it looks like it's about time to head out."

"Yeah ..."

"Don't slack off just because I'm not there. I'll be checking in with your teachers."

I whined.

He wrapped an arm over my shoulder and pulled me in for a hug. I leaned into him and hugged back. In the cold of the night he felt comfortably warm.

When we separated he reached into his bag, digging around. I heard a few clinks and he pulled out some coins.

"Here." He put them in my hand. "Go ahead and buy yourself a dessert."

"Thanks." I smiled sadly.

I stood there even after they all loaded up in the van and the back was shut. I watched the truck drive away, trying to make the day last a little longer in any way possible, but soon it was out of sight. He was gone, and I had to drag myself away from that spot.

I got back into the dining cart for the long ride back. I gazed blankly out the window while I idly stabbed and mushed up the dessert I bought. I absolutely had to graduate, no matter what.

Acknowledgements

I'd like to take a moment to thank my beta reader, my editor and my artist. Without their help I would never be able to publish a book of this quality.

I'm dedicating this book to my nephew, David.

Thank you to all of my readers. I truly appreciate your willingness to give my series a chance. From the bottom of my heart, thank you.

For more information about the Outlander Leander series, visit http://o-leander.com/.

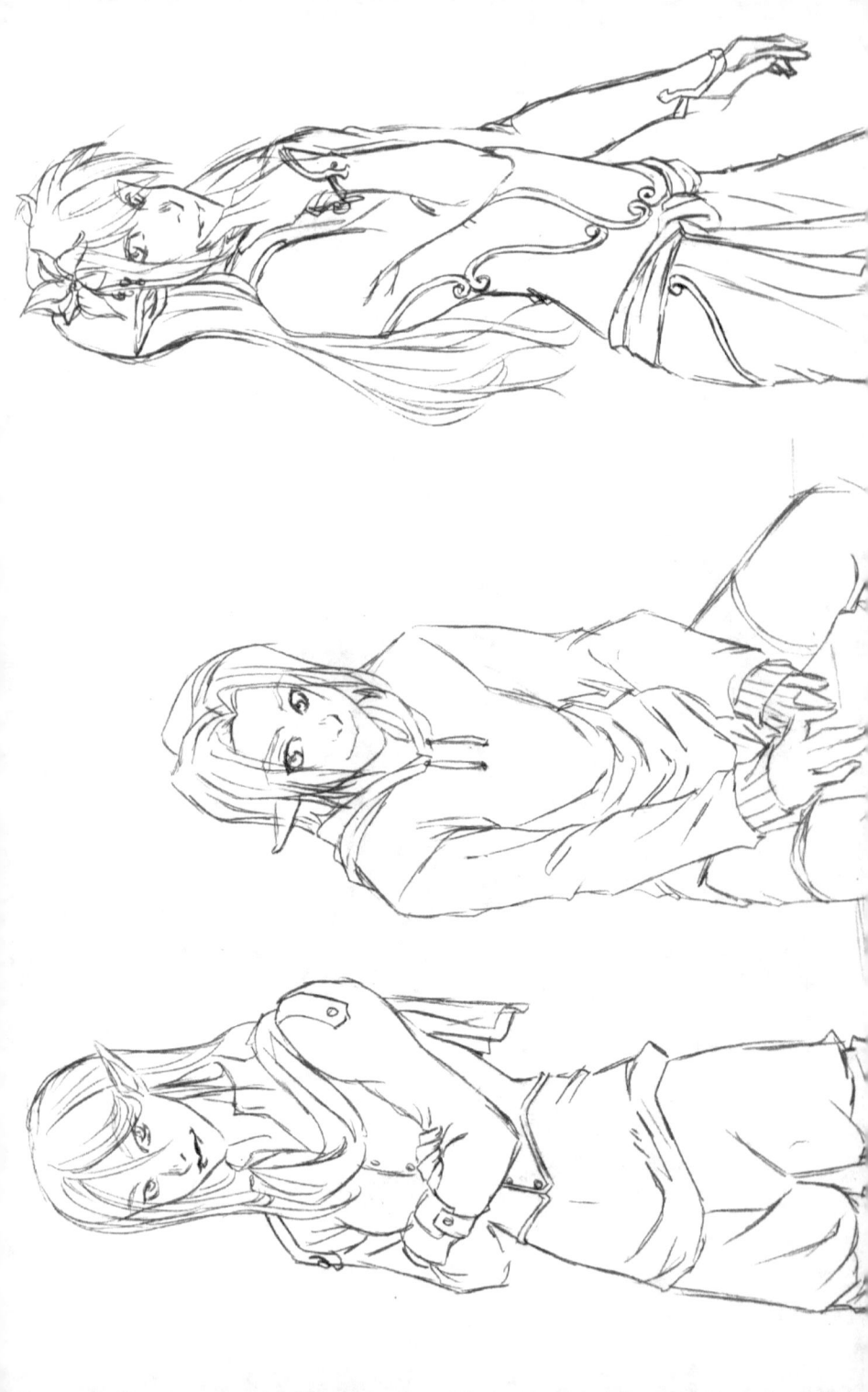